Death by Deinonychus

Written and Illustrated by

Scott E. Sutton

Action Publishing · Los Angeles

ISBN 13: 978-888045-54-3

Library of Congress Control Number: 2010942074
10 9 8 7 6 5 4 3 2 1

Action Publishing LLC
PO Box 391
Glendale, CA 91209

Visit us online at actionpublishing.com

TOP SECRET – SCIENCE LOG – DO NOT READ!

HALT! DO NOT READ THIS!
OFFICIAL SCIENCE TEAM ONLY! KEEP OUT!!

SCIENCE LOG #4
Written and Illustrated by –
Benjamin Banjo Montgomery
Photos by – Lee Wong
Computer Work by – Samantha Burke

SUBJECT – Our last trip through the doggy door time tunnel that is in our garage and goes back to the age of Dinosaurs which was created by a friendly-floating-robot-Alien librarian named Arbee and his assistant Zinzu, from the Planet Izikzah.

The tunnel was discovered by my Chow Chow dog, Dino.

I wish to announce our new secret Science Team members, but first the old members, which are …

Me, Banjo Montgomery – Team Paleontologist and Artist

My dog, Dino – Team Security

Lee Wong – Team Scientist and Complainer, ha, ha

And the new members are …

Samantha Burke – Team Computer Expert and Investigator and Arbee's Assistant

Bootsey, the Cat – Team Security Cat, Escape Artist and Attack Cat

CONGRATULATIONS! Welcome to the team. Remember, you are all sworn to SECRECY.

On our last trip through the doggie door time tunnel, Arbee had taken his time-traveling by starship back in time 80 million years ago to study Pteranodons. Those are flying prehistoric animals.

They lived on a small island we called Bird Island. We saw four or five different kinds of Pteranodons. It was awesome. These things were HUGE. They had wingspans of up to thirty feet.

I tried to touch one of their babies … which was STUPID … and its mom almost pecked my head off. I barely escaped, thanks to Arbee. Then, we almost got pecked to death AGAIN when one of the Pteranodons dropped a fish and I picked it up … which was SUPER STUPID.

Then Bootsey, Samantha's cat, snuck through the time tunnel, when he was not supposed to, AND somehow got out of the shuttle craft we locked him in. He shows up, steals the fish that fell on me and gets chased half-way around the island by psycho Pteranodons and almost gets eaten.

We chased that cat for HOURS, what a nightmare! We finally caught Bootsey, but then WE almost got eaten by a long-necked sea monster called an Elasmosaurus.

We shot it with the silver marbles from our slingshots that Arbee gave us to defend ourselves. They are cool because when you shoot a dinosaur with them, they go – FLASH – and the dinosaur falls asleep for fifteen minutes. It is awesome!

That night, when we were sleeping at our camp, two meat-eating dinosaurs snuck onto the island, and the next day we found a half-eaten dead dinosaur in the jungle which was very GROSS!

We explored Bird Island and saw two of the biggest Pteranodons that ever lived called Quetzalcoatlus.

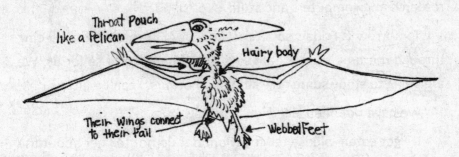

These things were 40 to 50 feet from wingtip to wingtip. They looked like giant prehistoric vultures. They were eating a dead dinosaur on the beach for lunch.

Then a meteor shower started and one hit the ground and the explosion was so big it knocked us on our butts.

So, we tried to run back to camp and leave Bird Island. That is when we ran into two miniature Tyrannosaurus Rexes who tried to eat us. We shot one with our slingshots.

Then, you will never believe this, Samantha's crazy cat Bootsey. That is right, he escaped AGAIN and jumped on the head of the second T-Rex and Dino goes and BITES the T-Rex's leg and they knocked it over.

It was CRAZY! Arbee zapped the T-Rex and we all escaped from Bird Island just as a huge meteor shower started to bomb us. That was a CLOSE ONE!

It has been two weeks since our last trip so Arbee has changed the time and location of his starship. We go back to see Arbee every two weeks.

Sam goes back more. She has been helping Arbee with his research and computers and stuff.

Tomorrow is Friday, so after school at 4:30 sharp, we are going through the time tunnel. Sam says Arbee has a surprise for us. We are going to study some new kind of dinosaurs. I can't wait!

We have not been killed yet ... luckily.

If I get eaten, please tell my Mom but do not tell her about the aliens because she will just think your some kind of kook and will not believe you and then she will call the police on you.

End of Science Log #4
Benjamin Montgomery

Chapter One
TONS OF TUNA CASSEROLE

Mr. and Mrs. Montgomery were standing in their kitchen, leaning against the counter eating pretzels. They were dressed in their "going out for a nice evening" clothes.

Mrs. Montgomery was speaking to Banjo Montgomery, her ten-year-old, red-haired, freckled-faced son. Samantha Burke, Banjo's cousin, and Banjo's best friend, Lee Wong were there, too. Also in the room were Sam's cat, Bootsey, Banjo's big, fuzzy Chow Chow dog, Dino, and Banjo's five-year-old sister, Cassie.

If Mr. and Mrs. Montgomery had known that Banjo, Lee, Sam, Dino, and Bootsey were actually members of a top secret Science Team that was working with time-traveling alien librarians from a planet one hundred light-years away, they would have been very upset. Actually, they would have freaked out. But they had no idea.

"Okay, listen up, you guys," said Mrs. Montgomery.

"Dad, and I, and Samantha's mom are going out to dinner and a concert, so we are going to be home late."

"How late?" asked Banjo.

"Probably after midnight," said Mr. Montgomery.

"Sam is the oldest, so she is in charge. Lee, your mother said you can sleep over. I have made dinner and some snacks, enough for everyone. They're in the fridge," said Mrs. Montgomery. "Make sure you keep the house locked. I want you all in bed no later than midnight. Any questions?"

"What if me and Lee want to play in the back yard?" asked Banjo.

"That's fine. Just don't leave the yard or the house," said Mrs. Montgomery. "And make sure the gate to the yard is locked. Remember, what Sam says goes. Got it?"

"Okay, Mom," said Banjo.

"Okay," said Sam. "No one leaves the house, keep it locked and everybody in bed by midnight. Oh, and there is food in the fridge. No problem."

"What about Cassie?" asked Banjo. Cassie did not know about the Science Team or the time tunnel going back to the Age of Dinosaurs, and for a good reason. If she ever found out, she would blab to everybody.

"Your sister is staying at her friend Janet's house for the weekend," answered Mrs. Montgomery.

"That's right, and my friend Janet has ... a ... swimming

8

"... pool, so I am going swimming and you're not," said Cassie to Banjo. Then she stuck her tongue out at him.

"Well ... whoop ... dee ... doo!" replied Banjo back to Cassie. "Man, she is so irritating!" he thought to himself.

"That's enough, you two," warned Mrs. Montgomery. "If you need anything call Lee's mom. You also have our cell phone number."

"Let's see ..." Mrs. Montgomery thought for a moment. "I guess that's it. You have fun, but behave while we are gone. Remember, we are trusting you to keep your promise. This is a big responsibility, and if you are good we will let you do this again. Okay?"

"Okay, Mom," said Banjo.

"I'll keep them in line," smiled Sam.

"Thanks, Sam," said Mrs. Montgomery, smiling back.

"Okay, we need to get out of here. Cassie, honey, go get your stuff and we will drop you off at Janet's ... hurry, hurry." She clapped her hands to get Cassie to move faster.

"Weee!" screamed Cassie. She ran from the kitchen, grabbed her bag and ran to the car in the garage.

"'Bye, kids," said Mr. Montgomery.

"'Bye, Dad, 'bye, Mom," said Banjo.

"'Bye," said Lee.

"Have fun," said Sam.

Mr. and Mrs. Montgomery grabbed their coats, got into the car with Samantha's mom and Cassie, and drove off, closing the garage door behind them.

"Perfect," said Banjo.

"No little sister," added Lee. "That's a good thing. I say we eat dinner before we crawl through the time tunnel to Arbee's starship. I am starved."

"Me, too," said Sam. "What did Momma Montgomery cook up for us?"

"Don't know," said Banjo. He walked to the refrigerator and pulled the door open. "Hmmm ... it looks like some kind of casserole ... could be tuna... I'm just guessing."

The three hungry kids stared gloomily at the big bowl of mystery casserole.

Dino trotted over and sniffed it. "Ruff," he snorted. "Fish, I hate fish," he thought.

"Fish, I'll eat it!" thought Bootsey the cat.

"Looks gross," Lee sighed. "What are those green things, peas?"

"Looks like it," said Banjo. "Guess Mom was in a hurry."

"I know ... what if we get Arbee to fix us something with his food computers?" suggested Sam. "Arbee loves being a chef and his food is the best!"

"Great idea," said Lee happily. "Arbee is a great cook."

"Cool," added Banjo. "Let's get our stuff and go."

The Science Team assembled in the Montgomery's garage and watched Banjo carefully replace the fake piece of the doggie door edge with the real metal piece. That way the time tunnel would not stay open all the time for others to discover and get lost in. It was the metal around Dino's dog door that caused the time tunnel to form.

"All set," said Banjo. He stepped back and – FLASH, POOF – a bright light came on in Dino's doggie door and it became the entrance to the time tunnel going back to the Age of Dinosaurs.

"So, I guess we are taking Bootsey," said Lee to Sam.

"Might as well," said Sam. "He will follow us anyway. I will put him on Arbee's ship where I can keep an eye on him. That's what I have been doing for the last two weeks and he hasn't caused any trouble."

"Good idea," said Banjo. "That cat can escape from anywhere. He should work for the CIA. We don't want what happened on our last trip to happen again. Bootsey almost got eaten four times by dinosaurs."

"Ha, ha, CIA cat," laughed Lee.

"It's a skill," thought Bootsey. He purred loudly as Samantha scratched him on the head.

"Woof," said Dino. "No fair, cat, you get to be carried, while I have to be on this leash," thought Dino.

"You're too big to carry," thought Bootsey. "Besides, cats

don't do leashes. Maybe you can be a cat in your next life."

"No, thanks," thought Dino. "Cats eat fish and I hate fish too much. I would rather come back as a poodle."

"Everybody in the tunnel," said Banjo.

They all crawled into the entrance of the time tunnel, disappearing into the far distant past.

The Science Team stood on one of the decks of a very large alien starship, after crawling out the other end of the time tunnel. This was unusual.

"Hey ... we are inside the ship," said Lee. "Usually we end up outside somewhere."

"Yeah," said Banjo. "What deck are we on, anyway?"

"You are on deck two," said a British-sounding voice from down the hallway. An oval-shaped alien with a yellow and red body floated over to Sam and the others.

"Hi, Arbee," said Sam.

"Hello, Samantha, good to see you. Hello, boys, and you too, Dino. And I see Bootsey has joined us again," laughed Arbee. "Well, it is probably better. You would find a way to follow Samantha, no matter what, eh, Bootsey, old boy?"

"MEOOWW," said Bootsey. "I like it here. The food's good and I like chasing those giant bird-lizard things."

"Well, that is just fine! Here is a biscuit for you and one

for Dino, too," said Arbee, handing them each a treat.

"So, Arbee, are you going to keep the entrance of the time tunnel in the starship now?" asked Banjo.

"Yes, we decided it would be safer there. That way, when you arrive, you will not be eaten by some Tyrannosaurus or Allosaurus. I should have thought of it earlier," explained Arbee.

"I like that idea a lot," exclaimed Lee. "If I get eaten, my mom will freak out."

"Also, if Bootsey or Dino came through, they won't get lost," added Sam, "like last time, especially since I come through every few days to help Arbee."

"Once every two weeks is plenty for me," said Lee. "There are too many things trying to eat you here."

"Well, who is hungry?" asked Arbee. "I am anxious to have you try my latest cooking creation."

"You read our minds," said Sam, "we are starved."

"So what did you make?" asked Banjo.

"You didn't make tuna casserole, did you?" asked Lee.

"No, but if you like, I could ..." Arbee was interrupted.

"NO!" said the boys.

"We have a year's supply of tuna casserole at home," explained Sam, laughing.

"Oh," replied Arbee. "Very well, let us go to the bridge

and see what I have cooked up."

They went to the ship's elevator and got in. They went up and in a few seconds – SWOOSH – The door opened and they were on the starship's control center, the bridge.

"Hello, everyone," said a squeaky voice. It came from another floating alien with eight eyes and eight arms who was in front of one of the starship's computers.

"Hi, Zinzu," they all said. Zinzu was the starships second-in-command.

"Ohhh," whispered Lee, "is that what I think I smell?"

"Is that fried chicken? Did you make fried chicken?" asked Banjo.

"It is fried chicken, with mashed potatoes and gravy, and peas with carrots," answered Arbee. "Come, this way."

He led them all to a small kitchen that he set up in a room next to the bridge. Arbee had also set up an eating area with a table and chairs.

"Here, everyone, sit." Arbee was very excited. He really liked cooking. He made them each a plate of steaming hot food from his food computer.

Arbee also made bowls of food for Bootsey and Dino. He made fish for Bootsey, steak for Dino, as usual.

"I like it here," thought Dino. "Maybe I will move in with Arbee and be an alien."

"This really smells good," said Sam. "It even looks like

fried chicken."

"Go ahead, taste it," said Arbee excitedly.

"Oh man, how good is this food?!" said Banjo.

"It's awesome," mumbled Lee, with his cheeks full of mashed potatoes.

"Thanks, Arbee," said Sam. "Your food keeps getting better each time you cook."

"Excellent!" said Arbee. "I am so glad you like it."

"You should open up your own restaurant," added Banjo. "Is this real chicken? It has bones and everything. Are you sure this isn't a real chicken?"

"It was created with the use of my food computer," said Arbee, "and it is healthier for you than the real thing, too!"

"Junk food that's good for you. That's a great invention." said Sam, laughing. "They should do this on our planet."

The kids ate everything on their plates. "Can I save some for later?" Banjo asked.

"Of course," said Arbee. He gave him a container to put some pieces of chicken in. Banjo eagerly stuffed the container full of chicken into his backpack.

"Arbee, you said we were going to study some new dinosaurs this time," said Banjo. "What kind?"

"Avery interesting species," said Arbee. "We are going so study ones that are sometimes referred to as … RAPTORS!"

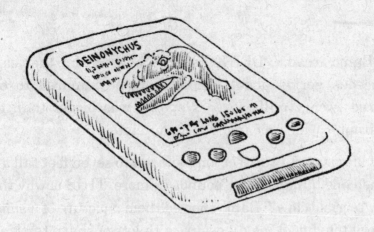

Chapter Two

OH WHERE, OH WHERE COULD THE RAPTORS BE?

"Raptors?" said Banjo. "You mean like, Velociraptors? But they lived in China and we are in North America."

"No," replied Arbee. "We are going to study the North American dinosaur that is similar Velociraptors called 'DEINONYCHUS'. It means, 'terrible claw'."

"Why did they call it that?" asked Sam.

"Whatever the reason, it can't be good!" said Lee.

Banjo pulled out his hand-held computer from his backpack. On it he had a Dinosaur Encyclopedia complete with pictures that he had downloaded into it.

"Here, take a look," said Banjo.

Everyone gathered around to get a look at the dinosaur on the small screen of his computer.

Banjo read, "DEINONYCHUS lived in the early Cretaceous period about, ummm ... one hundred to one hundred twenty million years ago. It was bigger than the Velociraptor which means, 'speedy predator'."

"It was about ten feet long and six to seven feet tall and weighed one hundred fifty pounds or more. THIS is why they call it 'terrible claw'," Banjo showed them a picture of a small, but very tough-looking dinosaur, with lots of sharp teeth.

"Look at its foot," said Banjo. "See the big curved claw, pretty awesome, huh?"

"Wow, that looks sharp," said Sam.

"Another meat-eating nightmare," Lee sighed.

"Hmm, very interesting," said Arbee.

"Paleontologists say it may have hunted in packs like wolves and used that big curved claw on its foot to slash its prey. They also said they may have been smart," said Banjo.

"Well, what did they mean by 'smart'?" asked Sam. "You mean like 'bird' smart or 'cat and dog' smart, or what?"

"I don't know," said Banjo. "But if it hunted in packs, well, that's pretty smart, I guess."

"None of these bird-lizards could be as smart as a cat," thought Bootsey, who was half-asleep in the corner with Dino.

"Or a dog," thought Dino. "A bird-lizard can't outsmart a dog. I have outsmarted lots of them."

Arbee took the computer from Banjo and read it for

himself. He thought for a moment. "I think we had better be very careful of these creatures," he said at last. "They are at the top of the food chain in this time period, which is not an easy thing to accomplish around here."

"On our planet, they made a movie about these things," said Lee. "In the movie, they were not only killers, but they were super-smart, I mean like ... scary-smart."

"Yeah, but that's just a movie," argued Banjo. "It's not real, they just made that up. It is just typical Hollywood junk."

"I hear what you are saying but I think being extra cautious would be a good idea," added Arbee, who sounded more concerned than usual.

"Maybe we should take a shuttle out and look around," suggested Banjo. "We can watch the Deinonychuses for a while and see what they are really like."

"That plan sounds safer," said Lee, "instead of running around in the bushes waiting for these things to slice us up with that big claw of theirs like a meatloaf."

"Agreed," said Arbee. "Let us take a shuttle out and observe them first."

They went toward the deck where Arbee kept his shuttle craft, the shuttle dock. "Which shuttle do you want us to take this time?" asked Banjo.

"We will take the bubble shaped shuttle, as usual," answered Arbee, as he pointed to a round shaped craft.

The bottom half of the shuttle craft was solid and the

top half was clear. It was good for watching dinosaurs. Arbee pushed a button on his chest and – SWOOSH – a door opened on the shuttle's side.

"Samantha, will you help me operate the shuttle?" asked Arbee.

"Sure," replied Sam. "Do you want me to record any dinosaurs we see, also?" she asked.

"Yes, but I will let you know which ones," said Arbee.

"Okay," said Sam.

Banjo and Lee would travel back to see Arbee every two weeks, but Sam, Banjo's cousin who lived in the Montgomery's guesthouse with her mom, came back through the time tunnel every two to three days.

Samantha's Dad was overseas working with the Air Force and her mom worked a lot, too. So Sam came back to see Arbee as often as she could. Arbee was teaching her about alien computers and researching things.

Sam was smart and a quick learner, which made her a lot of help. The time-traveling librarians could not remain in the past too long, or they would disappear after one year. So, the quicker Arbee could get his work done the better.

With everyone on board, including Bootsey and Dino, Arbee and Sam prepared to take off.

"Hold on," said Arbee, as he flew the shuttle craft down a short passageway and out a hatch into the sunny, cloudless prehistoric sky.

Arbee had parked the starship in a clearing on a flat topped mountain overlooking a big river valley. He flew away from the mountain and over the wide valley. The valley and surrounding hills were covered with thousands and thousands of bright green trees and flowering plants and ferns

"Hey, these trees look like regular trees," mentioned Banjo, "not palm trees and stuff, more like oak trees."

"Many of these trees you see in this forest you will find living on Earth in the present, such as oak, fig, and magnolia trees," said Arbee. "There are even pine trees in the higher mountains."

"There are also lots of ferns covering the ground," said Lee, whose nose was pressed up against the glass. "How hot is it out there, anyway?" he asked.

"About ninety-five to one hundred degrees at mid-day," answered Arbee. "You might find it a bit uncomfortable."

"Phew, one hundred!" sighed Lee. "Boy, you're not kidding. It seems like the temperature was hotter back in these times!"

"Hey, Arbee, there are dinosaurs!" interrupted Banjo. "Over there in that clearing."

Arbee flew the shuttle craft over the clearing that Banjo had pointed to.

"It looks like a small herd of something," said Sam. "Do you want some photos, Arbee?" she asked.

"Please, Samantha," said Arbee.

"Okay," she replied, and proceeded to push some buttons on the shuttle's control board – CLICK, CLICK."

"What are those things?" asked Lee. "They look like some kind of 'Spikeysaurus'."

Waddling slowly through the thick green ferns was a small group of ten or twelve large four-legged armored dinosaurs. Their backs were covered with lots of hard bony bumps, and along their sides were rows of sharp spikes or horns. They did not have a bony club on the end of their tails like their later ancestors would have.

"I wonder what all that armor is supposed to protect them from?" wondered Sam.

"You can be sure that whatever it is that it could eat us up like a kid eats a cookie," mumbled Lee.

"I think these dinosaurs are called 'SAUROPELTA'," said Banjo, as he looked at the dinosaur book on his computer. "It's the only armored dinosaur that lived around here in this time period. Man, look at the size of those things!"

"The biggest ones in the herd measure twenty-five feet," mentioned Arbee.

"They are as big as an army tank," added Lee, "big brown dinosaur tanks."

Dino jumped up to get a better look. "Hey, Bootsey, look at these giant thorny things," he thought.

Bootsey jumped on the control board to look. "I tell you everything is huge around here. What kind of food are they

feeding these things?" thought the cat.

"They eat leaves and weeds, junk like that," thought Dino, "like big cow-lizards."

"Humph, cows with spikes," Bootsey thought. "What will they think of next?"

Arbee laughed at what Dino and Bootsey were thinking. "Cows with spikes, indeed!" he said. Arbee could communicate with animals and other life forms with thought.

Arbee flew the shuttle off, toward the wide, green river that ran through the valley.

"Arbee, the computer sensors show that there is a big herd of dinosaur over by the river," said Sam.

"Yes, I see them now," said Arbee. "They looked like a smaller version of a long-necked plant eater. But their necks were shorter and their heads were longer."

They were small for a dinosaur, maybe a little taller than a man. Their skin was brown with dark brown splotches on their backs and dark tan under their chins and on their bellies. The babies were brown, too, with white spots on their backs. The babies were walking in the middle of the herd.

"Tenontosaurus," said Banjo, "that's what those are, I am pretty sure. The picture in this book isn't very good. It has the wrong colors and stuff."

The large herd was moving down the river eating ferns and drinking as they went along.

"Wonder where they are going?" said Lee.

Arbee flew the shuttle over the herd of Tenontosaurs, across the slow-moving river, and along the opposite side. Sam shot some photos of them as they went.

"Sam, do you see any sign on the computer sensors of any other dinosaurs?" asked Arbee. "I was hoping we would find a Deinonychus or two before the day is over."

"Nothing so far," said Sam. "There are some smaller animals, but nothing big enough to be a Deinonychus."

"Very well, we shall continue looking," Arbee sighed.

Arbee flew the shuttle craft along the river for a few more miles. He flew into some different parts of the forest as well, but still no Raptors could be found anywhere. Lee and Banjo were straining their eyes trying to find a Raptor but saw nothing, not even a footprint.

"Well, this is the first time we haven't been able to find a meat-eater," said Lee. "Usually the place is crawling with them and we have to fight them off."

Suddenly, Banjo yelled, "STOP ... Arbee, go back to that little bay on the riverbank. I swear I saw something by the river's edge down there."

Arbee turned the shuttle back and flew over the small bay along the riverbank Banjo had pointed to.

"See it? Right there, half-buried in the mud," said Banjo. "It looks like a Deinonychus and I am not sure but I think that it's ... dead."

Chapter Three
DEAD DEINONYCHUS

Arbee floated the shuttle craft over the body of a Deinonychus lying on its side by the edge of the river. It was not moving, part of its tail was in the water and some of its body was covered with mud.

"Arbee," said Sam, "the computer sensors show that thing is dead, like Banjo said."

"Okay," said Arbee. "Do the sensors show any other large life signs in the area?"

"Nope," replied Sam, "they just show some birds or Pteranodons in the trees, but nothing else."

"All right," said Arbee, "then we will go down and take a closer look at it. This may be the only chance we have to get a close look at one of these creatures."

Arbee landed the shuttle on the river bank about twenty feet from the Deinonychus's body. Sam checked the sensors one more time.

"It's still all clear," said Sam.

"Good," said Arbee. "The last thing we need is to get attacked by a pack of Deinonychuses. Do you boys have your slingshots and the flash marbles I gave you?"

"Yep," said Banjo.

"Right here," answered Lee.

"Good. I want you to load them and be ready, just in case," said Arbee.

"Loaded and ready," said Banjo.

"I am ready, too" added Lee.

Arbee had given Lee and Banjo flash marbles to use with their sling shots for protection from attacking dinosaurs. When they fired a flash marble at a dinosaur, it would do just that – FLASH – and knock the animal out for fifteen minutes.

"I'll hold Dino's leash," said Sam, "and I have got a surprise for Bootsey, the escape artist." Sam pulled out a short leash. "This is for you, you little monster."

Dino wagged his tail and had a big dog smile on his face. "I thought you said that cats don't do leashes, well, guess what, ha, ha."

"REEOWW," complained Bootsey. "Such an insult," he thought. But Sam grabbed the unwilling cat and put the leash on him. Bootsey was very unhappy. Samantha had both

Dino's and Bootsey's leashes. She tied them together so she would have a hand free to shoot photos for Arbee.

"I don't know about tying those two leashes together," mentioned Banjo, shaking his head. "If Dino takes off running, Bootsey is going to be road kill."

"Forget that!" thought Bootsey. He pulled his head out of the collar, jumped up onto Dino's back and laid on him like he was holding onto a fuzzy horse.

"WOOF," barked Dino in protest. "Hey! What am I ... a horse?" he thought.

"A little more fur off your back won't hurt you," thought Bootsey. "Start walking and stop talking. I am not getting down."

"Sometimes I hate being a dog," thought Dino. "We have to put up with so many insults."

"Looks like that problem is solved," said Arbee. "You are a good sport, Dino. Off we go. Samantha, get the door, will you?"

Sam pushed a button on the shuttle's computer control board and – SWOOSH – the door opened. The first thing the Science Team was greeted with was the harsh mid-day heat. It was dry, but hot.

"Geez, it must be a thousand degrees out here," complained Lee, fanning himself. "Now I know what a baked potato feels like."

They all walked over to the dead dinosaur. Sam shot

some photos while Arbee examined the animal.

"Ahhh, what a lovely smell," Banjo joked, "the sweet smell of stinky dead dinosaurs."

Dino snorted and hung back. "You sure that thing is dead? I don't trust it, not for a second," he thought.

"Of course it's dead," thought Bootsey. "Can't you smell it?"

"Do not worry, Dino," said Arbee. "Bootsey is right, it is definitely dead."

"So what killed it?" asked Lee. "I don't see any bites or cuts on it."

"It looks as if this animal may have died of old age," said Arbee. "It has been dead for maybe five or six days. It is a male, but I have no way of telling its age."

Banjo compared the picture of the Deinonychus on his computerized dinosaur book with the real one in front of him.

"Boy, this one has a lot more muscles than the one in the book, and look at this claw on his foot." Banjo touched it, and so did the others. "It's huge," he added.

"It's like a curved knife," whispered Lee. "That thing could slice you up like a watermelon."

"Very effective weapon, I should think," said Arbee.

"Also, this Deinonychus had totally different colors than the one in the dinosaur book, too," Banjo added.

The end of its nose and head was a dirty-mustard color. The rest of its head to halfway down its neck was a faded red color. Then the rest of its body was dark brown with dirty-mustard-colored stripes, and its belly was the same. But there was something else, something that paleontologists had wondered about.

"Arbee, check this out!" exclaimed Banjo. "It's got some kind of covering, like feathers. This thing is like a killer bird!"

"Yes, it is very interesting," replied Arbee, as he ran his hand over the short, feathery coat. "This animal is similar to a bird."

"The colors make it hard to see in the dirt," noticed Sam.

"Good camouflage for sneak attacks, I'll bet," said Lee, who was now standing guard with his slingshot. He was afraid they would be attacked at any minute. "Who would have thought that these things were monster-killer-birds, with stripes like tigers?"

"Arbee, how come this thing has been here for this long, but nothing is eating it?" asked Banjo. "I mean there should be some scavengers other than bugs?"

Arbee thought for a moment. "That is a very interesting question," said Arbee. "Hand me a sample container, will you, Sam?"

Sam put her camera down and got a plastic container out of her bag. "Here you go," she said.

"Thank you," Arbee said. He floated over to the head of the creature and took a sample of the claw, skin, feathers, and saliva and skin from the inside of its mouth.

"When we get back to the starship, maybe an analysis of this material will tell us why nobody wants to eat this dead dinosaur," said Arbee. "Let us get back aboard the shuttle and see if we can find some live ones before the sun goes down."

The team got aboard the shuttle craft.

"Ahhh, it's nice and cool in here," sighed Lee.

"Air conditioning is the best," thought Dino.

"Definitely," thought Bootsey as he jumped off of Dino's back. "Thanks for the ride."

Banjo was staring at the Deinonychus from the shuttle craft. He laughed.

"What's so funny?" asked Lee.

"Someday some paleontologist is going to dig this guy up and put him in a museum. He is probably already in a museum right now. We are seeing a fossil being made right at the start. It's kind of weird," said Banjo.

Arbee flew the shuttle back down the river in the direction of the big Tenontosaurus herd.

"So, where are we going to look now?" asked Banjo.

"Where there is prey," said Arbee, "there must be predators."

By this time the herd of Tenontosaurs was grazing along the river in front of the flat topped mountain near the starship. Arbee flew the shuttle into the forest near the herd.

"This is most unfortunate! There are still no Deinonychus," mumbled Arbee.

He flew closer to the base of the mountain.

"There is a bunch of caves at the bottom of the mountain," said Banjo. "Maybe they are hiding in there, if we look inside them ..."

"WHAT? Are you crazy!" interrupted Lee. "That is a perfect place for a surprise attack on us. You might as well serve yourself on a plate!"

"NO ... I mean, look in the caves with computer scanners, goof ball," argued Banjo. "I am not that dumb! Relax for two seconds, will you?"

"Arbee," interrupted Sam, "I have something here."

"On your sensors?" he asked excitedly.

"No, look on the ground in that clearing," said Sam, as she pointed.

They all peered through the glass at what appeared to be a pile of bones and dried skin. Arbee flew in for a closer look.

"Looks like the remains of a plant-eater, a Tenontosaurus," he said. "It probably was a member of that herd by the river."

"Another dead dinosaur," said Banjo. "Did this one die of old age too?"

"Plant-eaters don't die of old age in this place," said Lee, "just the meat-eaters."

"We will have a look," said Arbee, and he gently set the shuttle craft down.

"Anything on the sensors?" he asked Sam.

"Just the herd of plant-eaters toward the river," answered Sam. "But the sensors are not reaching into the caves."

"Sometimes the computer sensors have trouble looking underground if there are certain metals there," explained Arbee. "That is probably why we cannot see into the caves. But just to be safe, Banjo, you and Lee stand guard. We will leave Dino and Bootsey in the shuttle this time."

Arbee opened the shuttle door and they got out to investigate.

"Glad I am not going out there again," thought Bootsey.

"Me, too," thought Dino. "It's hot, too hot for furry dogs like me. It's just another dead lizard thing, anyway."

"Boring," thought Bootsey. "I guess mice haven't been invented yet. There is nothing good to chase around here." Bootsey yawned and stretched out for a nap.

When the Science Team got to the carcass it was very clear to everyone that this dinosaur had not died of old age. Sam took some photos and started pointing out clues like she was solving a murder case.

"I think this one was eaten. See all the footprints around the body? And you can still see the drag marks on the ground coming from the forest over there. I guess those are teeth marks on the rib bones," Sam said as she walked in a circle around the dead beast, swatting the thousands of bugs out of her face.

"Definitely," whispered Banjo. "They totally tore the thing to pieces."

"I got a bad feeling about this place," Lee whispered, looking around nervously.

"These tracks head off in the direction of those caves at the bottom of the flat topped mountain," said Banjo. "Maybe that's where we will find the Deinonychus."

Arbee had been busy examining what was left of the creature. "This animal was killed and devoured over a week ago," he said at last.

"Maybe the Deinonychus migrated somewhere else. I mean ... maybe they move around and follow the herds or something," said Lee. "I hope," he thought.

After collecting some samples, the team walked back to the shuttle craft. Banjo took out a piece of the fried chicken that he had saved and started eating it.

"Banjo, that's gross, how can you eat that now," said Lee, "after seeing that dead dinosaur?"

"Because ... I ... am ... hungry," replied Banjo, with a

mouth full of chicken.

As they neared the shuttle, Dino started barking excitedly at something.

"What's bugging him?" asked Lee.

"Probably wants my chicken," said Banjo. "He hates it when I eat food and don't give him any."

"He is not barking at you, Banjo," said Sam. "He is looking over there. Oh ... not good ... Arbee ... I think we found what we were looking for."

There on the edge of the forest, near the caves, was a pack of Deinonychus, and they were running straight for the Science Team.

Chapter Four
MEET SCARFACE

A group of Deinonychus stood at the entrance to their cave, overlooking the river valley. Their cave was underneath the same flat-topped mountain where Arbee's starship was.

The whole mountain had many of these caves and the Deinonychus pack controlled them all. This is where they laid their eggs and raised their young, slept, and planned their attacks. The caves had been home for Deinonychus for over fifty generations.

But now, the Raptors saw something they had never seen before, something very strange. They had just woken up from their mid-day nap and were grooming themselves, preparing to go out for the usual afternoon hunt, when they saw a large, round thing come out of the sky and land right in their territory.

After that, some unusual creatures got out of the round thing and were looking at the remains of an animal they had killed and eaten a week ago.

Why would they do that? The Raptors had consumed everything that was edible. There was not even enough left for the beetles and flies to eat.

"ERK ... ERK ..." A female barked a call and another Deinonychus came to the front of the cave. The others in the pack moved aside to let him through. He was the pack leader.

He had the faded-red face like the others, except he had a dark yellow stripe of color going down both sides of his face. It looked like a scar, but it was only a birthmark.

The scar-faced dinosaur watched the strange creatures with curiosity. But when one of the creatures looked and pointed towards the caves where he and his pack lived, he growled. Was that a threat? Yes ... to him it was a threat, to them and their home!"

"ERRR, ERK, ERK, ERK!" Scarface barked a command for the others to follow him. They must attack and drive out or kill these invaders.

Raptors had to constantly fight to maintain their position in the food chain in this world and they could not let any challenge go unanswered.

Dino and Bootsey had been watching Arbee and the others poking the dead dinosaur's remains.

"People are very odd," thought Bootsey. "What could

they possibly want with this dead lizard thing?"

"I do not know," thought Dino. "It smells bad and you can't eat it. People have no sense, I think."

It was Bootsey who saw them first. "Dino, over there in those trees," he thought. "Do you see them?"

Dino looked and whined. "They are more of those bird-lizard things, only these are alive and there is a whole pack of them," he thought.

"Well, don't just stand there, sound the alarm," thought Bootsey.

"ARF, ARF, ARF!" Dino barked loudly trying to warn Banjo and the others. Banjo looked up but did not see what Dino was barking at.

"Why don't people ever pay attention," thought Bootsey. "Keep barking, Dino. Sam, look over here, Sam, come on!"

Finally, Sam and Arbee looked at Dino then looked at what Dino was barking at. The Science Team started running when they saw the Deinonychus coming after them. Banjo dropped his chicken and he, Lee, Arbee, and Sam swiftly ran for the safety of the shuttle craft.

SWOOSH – Arbee opened the door. "QUICK! INSIDE!" he yelled and – SWOOSH – the door closed with everyone aboard. He rushed to the controls and flew the craft quickly off the ground.

"They were almost to the ship," yelled Banjo.

Sam managed to shoot some last-second photos of the charging pack.

The shuttle was almost ten feet off the ground when the pack leader leaped into the air with his feet and claws in attack position – WHAM – the scar faced Deinonychus hit the shuttle craft, making it the whole ship tremble. He fell back to the ground and got up snarling. Others in the pack were circling to attack from different directions.

"AAAAH!" Lee and Banjo screamed and fell to the floor after the impact.

Sam and Arbee were hanging on to the control board to keep from being bounced around.

"Samantha, turn on the camouflage-screens, now!" yelled Arbee.

Sam hit some buttons on the control board and – POOF – the Raptors stopped their attack when the shuttle craft vanished in mid-air.

Scarface made a barking call and the other Raptors spread out, searching the area to make sure the invaders were not hiding in the forest. When they were done they came back and with a series of clicks, barks, and chirps, told Scarface that the strange creatures were gone. The attack was successful and their home was safe.

"EERRK!" Scarface's mate called to him, she had found something on the ground.

Scarface came to investigate.

"Well, I hope you guys are happy, "said Lee. "You wanted some Deinonychuses and they almost made human hamburgers out of us."

"These guys are crazier than a Tyrannosaurus," mumbled Banjo. "Did you see how far off the ground that thing jumped?"

"I don't think they are crazy, Banjo," said Sam, "I think they are smart and organized. Did you see them signal to each other and attack from different directions?"

"It is as I thought," said Arbee, "these creatures are not like the other dinosaurs. They are quite a bit more intelligent than the other types we have studied so far."

They all watched the Deinonychus pack from the safety of the shuttle craft which was higher up in the air and could not be seen.

Dino looked down and growled. "These bird-lizards are bad, Bootsey," he thought. "They are not like the others."

"Smart bird-lizards," thought Bootsey. "What will they think of next?"

"Arbee, they are looking at something on the ground," said Lee.

"Yes, I see," replied Arbee. "It looks like … Banjo, did you drop a piece of chicken down there?"

"Yeah, I did. Why? Hey, those crazy raptors got my fried chicken!" complained Banjo.

"If you want to go back down and get it," said Lee, "then go right ahead. I will wait here for you."

Arbee and the others watched as the pack gathered around to investigate the strange object on the ground.

"The one with the mark on his face appears to be the pack leader," said Arbee. "That is interesting."

"Is that a scar on his face, or what?" asked Banjo.

Sam picked up her camera and hit "magnify" to get a better look. "No ... it's not a scar or a slash. It's just like a mark or something," she said.

"Scarface," said Banjo, "that's what I am calling that guy ... Scarface."

"Look at this, that Scarface guy is eating your chicken," said Lee.

The dinosaur scooped up the chicken, chomped it several times, and swallowed. He licked his lips afterwards. then he looked around for more chicken.

"Hey, Arbee, even dinosaurs like your cooking," laughed Sam.

"Well, it is finger-licking good," laughed Lee.

"Those dinosaurs stole my chicken," mumbled Banjo. "I wonder if he knows he is eating his cousin from the future, ha, ha, ha! The joke is on him!"

"Do not worry, Banjo," answered Arbee. "There is more chicken where that came from." Arbee smiled and thought to himself. "Hmm, even dinosaurs liked my cooking."

They watched the pack for a while longer.

Suddenly, Scarface barked and the pack grouped together and ran back to their home in the cave.

"I think we have seen enough for today," said Arbee. "I want to study the data we collected so far. Samantha, turn off the camouflage-screens. We are going back to the starship. We will study them again tomorrow."

CLICK – "Screens off," said Sam.

Arbee and the team flew off to the top of the mountain and back to the safety of the starship. But the Science Team aboard the shuttle craft did not realize that they were being watched.

Hidden in the forest, Scarface and his mate saw the round flying thing appear again and fly over their heads and to the flat topped mountain above. The two Deinonychus had done an old Raptor trick to get an enemy to show themselves by pretending to leave. The trick worked beautifully. Not only did they make the strange creatures show themselves, but Scarface knew where they were going, as well.

There was something else. Those creatures had left some sort of food he had never eaten before. It was excellent! It was not the taste. Taste did not mean much to a dinosaur. But animals can sense when something is healthy for them, and this food was better than anything he had ever eaten. It had something in it that their bodies needed. It was far better than having to tear through the tough hide of a Tenontosaurus.

"ERK, ERK, ERRRK," barked Scarface. He called to the pack and led them running quickly into the caves. They knew where everyone of these caves went to.

Using their excellent night sight and sense of smell, they ran deeper and deeper into the passageways under the mountain.

The pack did not understand. What was Scarface doing? What were they after? This was certainly a strange hunt they were on, but survival in a Deinonychus pack meant they had to work as a team.

A single Deinonychus would find it hard to get by in this very hostile world of theirs, having to live off of small animals and bugs or even dead animals.

Scarface had taken over for an older male a few months ago. He was a good leader, who always found the best dinosaurs to eat, so the pack rarely went hungry these days.

The old Raptor that Scarface replaced became so old that he could no longer hunt. Eventually could not eat either, even though the pack brought him food. Raptors took care of their old ones up to a point.

When he knew his time was coming to an end, the old one wandered off to die in peace, just as his ancestors had done for thousands of years.

The Deinonychus pack did not eat each other, or their

45

young ... for a reason.

After a short time of running through the endless caves, Scarface and the pack came to an exit at the crest of the flat topped mountain.

They looked up just in time to see the round flying thing disappear into a clump of trees.

"EEEE, ERK," barked Scarface. It was the signal that the hunt was on. The pack ran like the wind towards a clump of trees and the unsuspecting Science Team.

The raptors were ready to eat and these creatures in the round flying thing had the food that they wanted.

Chapter Five
POISON RAPTOR

When the Science Team got back to the starship everyone was hungry. It had been a long day.

"I am starved," said Banjo. "When do we eat?"

"Well, what would you like?" asked Arbee happily. "Would you like more chicken?"

"Yes!" said Banjo. "More fried chicken!"

"Say, 'please', Banjo," whispered Sam

"More fried chicken … pleeeease," Banjo joked.

"Can I have meat loaf?" asked Lee. "Please?"

"Not a problem," answered Arbee. "What about you, Samantha, what would you like?

"Boy, I could sure go for a chicken salad with avocado dressing, please," she answered. "Can you make that?"

"But of course I can," said Arbee, rubbing his hands together. "I love a challenge." For some reason Arbee really liked being a chef and making good food.

While Arbee cooked up dinner, Sam took all the samples that they had collected on their research tour and, with Zinzu's help, put them in the ship's testing computer. Lee and Banjo helped her.

Then she downloaded all the pictures she had taken into another computer. This computer she was using would make a copy of everything so that when Arbee flew his ship back into present time, his research pictures would not disappear.

Time travelers learned that you cannot take things out of the time they belong in or they will vanish. That includes taking photos or videos, but you could take computer-made copies of photos or videos.

The rule was that you cannot take a thing or a direct copy of that thing out of the time where it belongs.

"Dinner is served," called Arbee.

The kids dropped what they were doing and ran to Arbee's temporary kitchen.

Bootsey and Dino were happily eating their meals.

"It smells awesome," said Lee.

"Meat loaf, mashed potatoes, and peas for you, Lee," said Arbee. "And we have fried chicken, mashed potatoes and peas with carrots for Banjo. And Samantha, here is your chicken salad with avocado dressing."

"Wow, you did it," said Sam, laughing. She took a taste. "Oh … my… gosh, it's perfect! It's better than perfect!"

"Oh, Banjo, I made some extra chicken for you to snack on later," said Arbee.

"Tank yoo," mumbled Banjo, whose cheeks were stuffed with food.

"You know Arbee … you should open a restaurant because THIS is seriously the best food I have ever eaten," said Lee.

"Well … thank you Lee," replied Arbee.

The Science Team did not say a word until every scrap of food was finished. Banjo packed his extra chicken into a plastic container and stored it in his backpack.

"Burrrp!" went Banjo. "Well, excuuuse me. That food was so good," he said.

Zinzu floated up next to Arbee. "Well, it seems your food has made quite an impression. They ate it like they were starving!"

"It is not just the flavor," whispered Arbee to Zinzu. "I believe that this is the first meal they have eaten that had all the vitamins and minerals their growing bodies require. They are craving high-quality food, not just good taste."

"Hmmm," replied Zinzu. "They act as if they had not eaten in days … I do not understand why."

"I believe there is something wrong with planet Earth's

food supply," Arbee went on. "It is most alarming."

"Let me do some research on this," said Zinzu quietly.

"Yes, that would be good then let me know what you find out," whispered Arbee.

"Okay, I will let you know," said Zinzu. He flew off to a computer on the other side of the bridge.

Instead of feeling sleepy after dinner, Lee, Sam, and Banjo felt more alert and energetic. Dino and Bootsey were taking their usual after meal naps.

"Arbee, we have scanned all the photos and entered all the samples into the computer," said Sam.

"Thank you," said Arbee. "Gather around, everyone. Let us look at what we have learned today, shall we? Samantha, I want a look at the pictures we took to start with."

"Okay, here goes," said Sam. She pushed three buttons on a computer board and on a large screen the video of what they had seen that day appeared.

"There are the armored dinosaurs," said Lee.

"Sauropelta," corrected Banjo. "And there is the Tenontosaurus herd. Hey, Sam, these are good shots!"

"Thanks," said Sam, who was a little embarrassed.

"There is the dead Deinonychus," said Arbee. "And what does the computer have to say about the samples we took off of the body?"

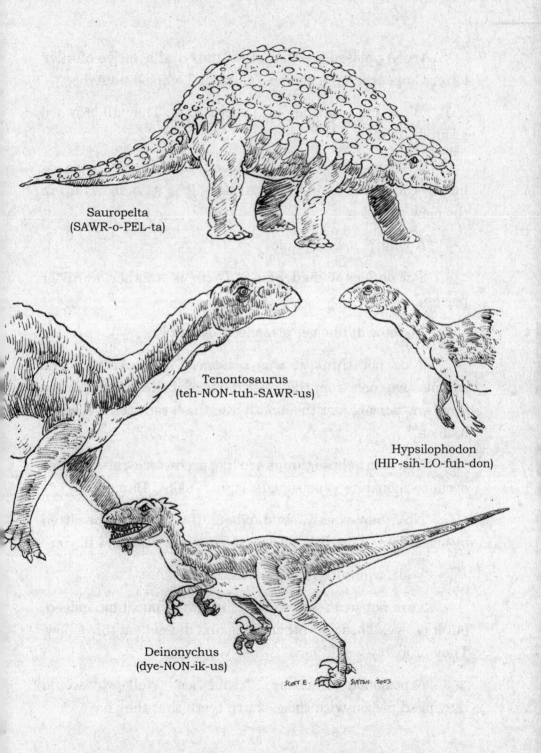

Sauropelta
(SAWR-o-PEL-ta)

Tenontosaurus
(teh-NON-tuh-SAWR-us)

Hypsilophodon
(HIP-sih-LO-fuh-don)

Deinonychus
(dye-NON-ik-us)

SCOTT E. SUTTON 2003

Arbee pressed a series of buttons and a series of alien letters appeared on a screen. "Curious," whispered Arbee.

"What did you find out?" asked Sam. They all crowded around the screen.

"It seems that the saliva and tissue samples from its mouth contain a toxin," said Arbee. "It is also shows up in the claw samples."

"A what?" asked Banjo

"Poison," explained Sam. "Toxin is another word for poison."

"So, how did he get poisoned?" asked Lee.

"I do not think it was poisoned," said Arbee. "The samples we took from the other parts of its dead body do not have any poison, just the mouth and the large attack claw on its foot."

"You mean these things are like prehistoric rattlesnakes because their bite is poisonous, right?" asked Banjo.

"No ... not exactly," said Arbee. "If you were to be bitten by one and managed to survive, this toxin would not kill you."

"Well, what does it do?" asked Banjo.

"I am not sure," said Arbee. "It is very puzzling, indeed, but it does explain why other dinosaurs did not eat this fellow. They probably would have gotten very sick."

"A poisonous dinosaur ..." said Lee. "Well, why would they need poison with those sharp teeth that they have?"

"Samantha, please fast forward the film to where the Deinonychus pack attacked the shuttle craft," asked Arbee.

"Okay," said Sam. "Hold on, let me find it ... here it is."

The film started as the shuttle craft was lifting off the ground. Everything went by so fast that they could not clearly see what had happened. The Raptors charged, the pack split up, and Scarface made his leaping attack on the shuttle craft.

Everybody flinched at the part where Scarface slammed into the shuttle's glass cover.

"Whoa," whispered Banjo. "That was crazy!"

"Samantha, play it again, but in very slow motion this time," said Arbee.

"Okay," she said. "Here goes." She pushed some buttons.

Nobody was sure what Arbee was looking for. The film showed the pack running then ...

"There, you see it?" exclaimed Arbee. "Watch closely."

They all did, and what they saw frightened them.

Scarface was leading the charge and, as he did, he turned his head to the Raptors on the right and made a sound. Then he turned his head to the Raptors on the left and did it again. At that instant, two Raptors went running to the right, and two went running to the left. They were circling around to attack the shuttle from three directions.

"Oh man," whispered Banjo. "Scarface is telling the others what to do. They are talking to each other sort of like dolphins do, I guess."

"So much for the idea that dinosaurs were just stupid reptiles," said Lee. "Another paleontology theory bites the dust."

"These guys plan stuff," said Banjo. "Maybe Hollywood got it right after all."

"I believe that if these creatures had not gone extinct, that Deinonychus or one of its ancestors would be the number one life form on planet Earth, not humans," said Arbee. "Alright, Samantha, please store all this information in the computer's memory."

Sam pushed some buttons. "All stored," she said. "What should I do with all the skin, bone, and other samples we collected?" she asked.

"Oh, just dump them outside the starship. I do not want things from this time left in the ship. Lee, Banjo, run this down to deck one, call on the radio and Samantha will open the hatch to the outside for you."

"You don't mean go outside, do you?" asked Lee. "Isn't that dangerous?"

"I do not want you to walk around, Lee," said Arbee. "Just step outside, bury the samples, and come straight back. The Deinonychus caves are far from here."

"Okay," grumbled Lee.

"Come on, trust me, it will be fine," said Banjo, as he grabbed the sample containers and a small shovel. He and

Lee walked to the elevator and got in.

Banjo pushed the button to go to deck number one.

"Okay, I'll do this, but no wandering around," said Lee. "We will go out, dump the stuff then get back in the ship ... fast."

"No worries," assured Banjo. "Besides, it's nighttime, what's there to see out there?"

They got to deck one and walked to the hatch where Banjo pushed the radio button. "Sam, we're here, let us out."

"Okay," replied Sam. "Make it quick, and call me as soon as you're back inside so I can close up."

SWOOSH – The door opened. Lee flinched, expecting to be attacked by something, but there were no dinosaurs there that they could see.

"Lee, relax. See? There is nothing out there," said Banjo.

"Just let's hurry up," said Lee. He was scared, so scared that the hairs on the back of his neck were standing straight up.

The boys walked out into the warm night air. It was dead quiet. The only sound that could be heard was their footsteps on the rocky ground and the breeze rustling through the leaves in the trees.

Suddenly, there was a "SCREE, SCREE, SCREE" call, from a tree.

Lee jumped. "Oh, man, what was that?" he whispered.

"It was probably some Pterodactyl or something," said Banjo. "Don't be so jumpy."

With the little steel shovel that Arbee had given him Banjo dug a small hole and then he and Lee emptied the sample containers into it. They filled the hole in and kicked some rocks over it with their feet.

"Okay, let's go," said Lee.

Banjo did not show it, but he was scared, too. He felt like someone or something was watching him! They both ran back to the starship and through the door.

"Safe," Lee sighed. They started to walk back to the elevator. "Banjo, you forgot to close the door!" said Lee.

"Oh, yeah, no problem, we can use the radio in the elevator," said Banjo

They reached the elevator, got inside, and closed the door.

What Lee and Banjo had not seen was that they had been followed into the ship by a very quiet, very clever, and very hungry group of four ... Deinonychus.

Chapter Six
SNACK ATTACK

Scarface and the other Deinonychus had been searching for the Science Team's hideout for a long time without any success. Finally, Scarface's mate bumped into something strange.

It looked like a forest, but when she tried to walk into it, she could not get in. The others tried as well but the same thing happened. It was like a see-through wall was keeping them from getting into this part of the forest.

"EEE ... ERK," Scarface told the pack to spread out and try to get into the trees from different sides, but still, no luck.

For some reason there was a very large round section of forest that had an unseen wall around it that was keeping them out.

Scarface snorted. He knew those creatures that had the special food were in this forest ... somewhere, but how do they get in?

58

He stood for a moment scratching a bug bite on the side of his head, trying to figure out what to do next.

"EEE, ERK, ERK," he growled finally. He sent the pack around again to find a way in, and again they came back, and by making clicking and grunting noises told Scarface, "No way in."

The Raptors were chattering back and forth to each other trying to decide what to do next. It was dark now and the Raptors were getting even hungrier.

They were about to leave and find something else to hunt, when all of a sudden, an opening in the forest wall appeared out of nowhere. This surprised them and the pack quickly ran for cover so they would not be spotted.

Scarface and the others watched as two small and weak-looking creatures with strange skin walked out of the opening.

"Ah, ha, these were the same creatures they chased back in the clearing, the ones with the special food," he thought.

The creatures looked frightened. Scarface and the others could see the fear in their eyes. They had seen that look a thousand times before. The creatures were so scared that when one of the Deinonychus accidentally woke a sleeping Pterodactyl in a tree, the creatures jumped when it flew off into the night, screeching.

These two would be easy prey for a pack of Deinonychus. They might even be good to eat, but that would come later.

Scarface and the pack had to find that special food first. They watched as the small creatures dug a hole in the ground, buried something, and quickly scurried back into the opening in the forest.

It was now time for the pack to move in. Scarface made a low chirping sound, signaling three Raptors to follow him in and three to stay outside to stand guard. Without making a sound, Scarface and the others sneaked into the starship doorway. They immediately smelled the food they were looking for. At last they were in the right place.

This cave they were in was not like any cave they had been in before. For one thing, it was light inside, which made the pack nervous.

They sniffed the air for any sign of smoke or heat in case the light was caused by a fire, a deadly enemy of all dinosaurs. There was no smell of smoke or any sign of fire. So, the pack continued down the hallway, looking for the food.

By this time Banjo and Lee were safely inside the starship's elevator.

Banjo called Sam on the radio. "Hi, Sam," said Banjo. "We are done, so you can close the door now."

"Okay," replied Sam. She pushed some buttons closing the starship's outer door, not realizing that she had just trapped four Deinonychus inside the ship.

As soon as the ship's door slammed shut, the sound surprised the Raptors and they took off running. They ran down the hallway, up several ramps. Soon there were Deinonychus scattered on three decks of the ship. This set off a loud alarm that could be heard all around the starship.

"WARNING, WARNING, UNKNOWN LIFE FORMS HAVE ENTERED THE SHIP. WARNING, WARNING."

"What? What did I do?" asked Sam.

"Nothing, Samantha," said Arbee. "Some life form has entered the ship while the door was open. It is probably not serious. Zinzu, turn off the alarm, please."

"Alarm off," replied Zinzu.

"What is going on?" asked Arbee.

Zinzu checked his computer screen. "Sensors show four large life forms aboard. I am getting visual now," Zinzu said, as he pushed some buttons. "I believe they are the dinosaurs that you call ... Deinonychus, and they have managed to gain access to decks one, two, and three."

"WHAT? How did they do that?" said Arbee

"Arbee, Lee and Banjo are down on the lower deck," cried Sam. "They will be eaten!"

Suddenly, a voice came over the radio. "Hellooo up there," said Banjo.

"Banjo, this is Arbee. Where are you?"

"Well, Lee and I are sitting in an elevator and it is stuck," answered Banjo. "We have tried pushing all the buttons, but nothing is happening ... it won't go up."

"Phew," sighed Sam, "they are safe in the elevator."

"Should we just open the door and walk up to deck five or find another elevator that is working?" asked Banjo.

"Banjo, please listen to me very carefully," said Arbee. "Stay ... where ... you ... are. Do not ... I repeat ... DO NOT OPEN THE ELEVATOR DOOR."

"Okay, but, how come?" asked Banjo.

"There are FOUR DEINONYCHUS loose on the ship," answered Arbee.

"WHAT?" yelled Banjo.

"See, I TOLD you opening the door was a BAD IDEA. Oh, man, this is nuts!" Sam and Arbee could hear Lee yelling in the background.

"You two just stay where you are. The ship has locked all the elevators, that is why they are not working," explained Arbee. "You will be safe in there for now."

"Okay, we will stay here," said Banjo.

The alarm woke Dino and Bootsey from their after-dinner nap.

"What's all the noise?" thought Dino.

"It seems that some of those smart bird-lizard things have snuck onto the ship," thought Bootsey.

"Oh, great. I suppose the people let them in," thought Dino. "I hate fighting after I eat. It makes me throw up."

"Well, those things are on the ship whether we like it or not," thought Bootsey.

"Sometimes I hate being the dog," thought Dino. "I suppose we will have to help clean this mess up."

Bootsey and Dino went and stood guard by the bridge door. If they had to take on these bird-lizard things, it was going to be messy, but they would do it. That was their job ... to protect the silly humans when they do stupid things like let a pack of killer bird-lizards on the starship.

Arbee went into action. "Samantha, you stay on the bridge in case I need you. Zinzu and I have to get these animals off the ship before they do serious damage."

"Right," replied Sam. "But if one of those things comes up here, how do I defend myself? I don't have my slingshot."

Arbee went to a cabinet, opened it and took out something that looked like a flashlight.

"This is a hand blaster. It is set on paralyze. You just point and push this button here and it will knock out anything for a long time," explained Arbee. "Do not use it unless you absolutely have to, understand? And try not to hit any of the computers," he added.

"Okay," said Sam. "I'll be careful, I promise."

"I know you will," said Arbee. Arbee then floated over to Dino and Bootsey. "You two guard her," he commanded.

"Banjo and Lee are safe, so please guard Samantha."

"Woof," barked Dino. "That was our plan, somebody has to protect the people when they mess up," he thought.

"You two will do fine," said Arbee. "Zinzu we must go." Zinzu and Arbee flew off down the hallway to stop the Deinonychus invasion.

Banjo and Lee were sitting comfortably on the floor of the elevator. Banjo got up and went to the radio.

"Hey, Sam, so what's going on now?" he asked.

"I am watching the bridge with Dino and Bootsey while Arbee and Zinzu have gone to get rid of the Raptors. You guys just sit tight, okay?" she said. "I will let you know what to do when I know."

"Yeah, okay," sighed Banjo. Banjo flopped back on the floor and opened his pack. "Well, we got chicken and we got water, so, we are good."

"I am not hungry," said Lee. "I just hope those monsters can't get in here."

Banjo opened his container of fried chicken. "Yum, smells good," he said and then closed the lid. "No, not now, I'll save it for later. We may be in here for a while."

In the hallway outside of the elevator, Scarface caught the scent of the fried chicken. "ERK, ERK, ERK," he called to the others to come. His mate came running, but the rest of the pack was too far away to hear his call.

Scarface and his mate did not wait. They sniffed the air and followed the scent of the chicken until they got to the elevator door. Scarface growled. The food was here somewhere, he knew it. The two hungry Raptors started scratching and biting at the door, making deep scratch marks on the metal with the enormous curved claws on their hands and feet, but the door was too hard and too thick to claw through.

They kept scratching the door for a number of minutes but still it did not work. Then Scarface noticed some colored lights on the side of the door. He tried to bite them, but nothing happened.

Then he tried to scratch them with the sharp claws on his hands. Again nothing happened, until after some time he accidentally hit a yellow button and – SWISH – the elevator door opened.

Chapter Seven
RAPTORS, RAPTORS EVERYWHERE

Banjo and Lee felt like they were in a bad horror movie. Here they were, trapped in an elevator, while just outside the door who knows how many hungry Deinonychus were going crazy trying to bite, claw, and scratch their way in.

Lee decided, "I am not going to sit around and wait to be slashed to death by psycho poisonous dinosaurs. Sam, are you there?" asked Lee calling over the radio.

"Yeah, what's up?" she asked. "What is all that noise?"

"It's those stupid Raptors," Lee answered. "They are trying to get in here and I don't think the door is going to hold. Is there any way out of this elevator, like an escape hatch or something?"

"Lee, that door is made of alien metal," argued Sam. "There is no way ..."

"Tell it to the Raptors," interrupted Lee. "What happens

if they hit the 'open' button by accident? Find us a way out of here," he yelled, "and hurry."

"Okay, okay," said Sam. "Hang on, I'll check the computer."

As Lee and Banjo sat waiting to hear from Sam the Raptors were clawing even harder, trying to rip through the door.

"Lee, we have slingshots, we have flash marbles, let's just blast them," said Banjo.

"Banjo – five feet – remember?" yelled Lee. "Anything within five feet gets knocked out by the flash marbles. We ... are ... too ... close."

Banjo sighed, "Okay, I get it ... bad idea."

Lee stood next to the radio, waiting for Sam. "Come on, come on," he mumbled, as he nervously bounced up and down.

"Lee," Sam's voice came over the radio at last.

"Yeah," he said.

"There is an escape hatch," she said.

"Okay, where?" asked Lee.

"It's in the ceiling," said Sam. "Stand on the hand rail and you will see a red and yellow button."

"Yeah, yeah ... I see it," answered Lee.

"You have got to push both buttons at the same time. That will open the hatch," she explained. "Then, if you crawl up the ladder, you will get to the next higher deck. Okay?"

"Got it," said Lee. "Banjo, let's GO!"

"But, Lee," Sam said, "there are Raptors on decks one, two, and three ... Lee ... Lee, are you there?"

But Lee was not there. He and Banjo had already crawled through the hatch seconds before Scarface accidentally opened the elevator door. The only sound Sam heard was the roaring of Scarface as he and his mate burst into the empty elevator and growling.

Scarface sniffed the air. The smell of food was strong, very strong. They were getting closer. He bent down, smelled the floor and found a few crumbs. He lapped them up with his long tongue. Where did these creatures go with that food?

"EEK, ERRK," barked the other Raptor. She was looking at a hole in the ceiling. Scarface looked up and saw it as well.

They were familiar with caves and, to them, this was just another cave. The creatures they were after went through the hole in at the top of the strange cave.

Scarface and his mate ran out of the elevator and down the hallway. They would find a passageway to the higher part of the cave and get those creatures and the food.

Arbee and Zinzu went flying through hallways and

down ramps to get to deck three. Each of the five decks on the ship had four entrances, not including the elevators.

The trick was to try to guess which entrance the Raptors would use. Even with sensors, these things were hard to track. They moved so fast and this was a big ship!

Zinzu checked his hand-held sensor. "Life form at the end of this hallway," he said.

They flew to the end of the hallway, but there was nothing there.

"It has gone to deck four," said Zinzu.

"Quickly, this way," said Arbee, and they flew up the passageway. He pushed a button on his chest. "Samantha, come in, Samantha," he said.

"I'm here," she said.

"Stay alert, Samantha, there is a Raptor moving in your direction," Arbee warned her.

"Oh darn … okay, I'll be ready," she replied. Arbee could hear the fear in her voice. "Arbee … Lee and Banjo are not in the elevator anymore. They climbed out of the escape hatch."

"Escape hatch?" exclaimed Arbee. "Why did they leave?"

"The Raptors figured out how to open the door," she said.

"Oh, blast!" grumbled Arbee. "Samantha, I am sending Zinzu up to protect you and the bridge. Make sure you do not shoot him."

70

"I promise I won't shoot him," she said, "but, what about Lee and Banjo?"

"I will take care of them," said Arbee. He turned to Zinzu. "Zinzu, we must split up."

"Right," replied Zinzu, before Arbee could finish. "I will return to the bridge immediately." Zinzu zoomed off down the hallway.

"Whoever said that working in the history research department for the Galactic Library Service was a peaceful job did not know what they were talking about," mumbled Arbee, as he flew off to save the boys.

Lee and Banjo had crawled a long way through the inside of the ship until they found a hatch. It had some sort of alien numbers painted on it.

"I don't know Arbee's language," said Lee. "But I think this is a number '2' here."

"Well, let's try it," said Banjo.

"Wait," whispered Lee. "What if there are Raptors out there?"

Banjo sighed, "You may be right. Let's open the hatch slowly first," suggested Banjo, "and make sure it's all clear."

"Good idea," whispered Lee. "Try it."

Banjo pushed a button and the door opened slightly.

He looked out only to see a Raptor standing in the hallway sniffing around. It turned, saw the open hatch and charged.

SLAM – Banjo shut the door just in time. The Raptor was growling and scratching at the hatch door.

"Whoa, that was a close one," he said. "Okay, deck two is no good."

"Let's climb to deck three," said Lee. "Maybe it's clear."

"I hope so," said Banjo, and the two boys started the long climb up the ladder over pipes and electrical wires to deck three.

Back on the bridge, Sam was standing behind a computer control board for protection. She had the blaster out and pointed at the main entrance to the bridge.

Dino and Bootsey were by her side. But when the hair on Bootsey's back stood straight up, and Dino started to growl, Sam knew something was coming. She was so nervous she almost could not talk.

"Zi ... Zinzu, is that you?" she yelled.

It was not Zinzu. It was a Deinonychus. It crept slowly onto the bridge, making snorting noises and ruffling its feathers. It was sniffing the air like it was looking for something.

Dino started barking at it, but he did not charge it. "If I could just scare it off," he thought. "ARF, ARF, ARF!"

"Get OUT OF HERE, dinosaur! I will shoot you, I swear!" yelled Sam. She was trembling with fear, barely able to hold the blaster straight.

The Raptor looked over at Sam, Bootsey, and Dino, but did not attack. Instead, it ran straight for Arbee's kitchen.

Sam got up enough courage to sneak a look into the kitchen where she saw the strangest thing. "It is eating all of Arbee's fried chicken. What the...?" she whispered.

She was interrupted by something else coming into the room. Sam aimed the blaster at it.

"Do not shoot! It is I, Zinzu," said a squeaky voice.

"ZINZU!" Sam yelled. "Boy am I glad to see you!"

"And I am glad you are not hurt. Now, quickly, where is the dinosaur?" asked Zinzu.

Sam pointed to the kitchen. "It's in there."

Zinzu flew in. The Deinonychus roared and – ZAP – the Deinonychus was knocked out and on the floor.

"Got him," said Zinzu, "It was eating the fried chicken that Arbee had prepared ... that is odd!"

"I know," said Sam. "It didn't attack us, it went straight for the chicken. It's like he wanted the chicken all along."

Banjo and Lee finally made it to deck three.

"Okay, I looked last time," said Banjo. "It's your turn."

Lee shook his head and crept to the hatch. He unlocked it as quietly as he could and slowly opened it just a crack. He looked around some then opened the door a little more.

"What do you see?" whispered Banjo.

"So far, so good," reported Lee. "No Raptors."

"Oh, good!" whispered Banjo. "Are you sure?"

Lee opened the door all the way and looked to the right, then to the left, still no Raptors.

"All clear," he said, as he climbed into the hallway.

Banjo climbed out after him and quietly closed the hatch door. "Load your slingshot," he said, as he took his out.

Lee took out his slingshot and did the same. "We need to get to the bridge, fast," he whispered.

"Yeah, good idea," replied Banjo.

They ran down the hallway to get to deck four but ... as they rounded a corner, they almost crashed right into the back of a Raptor who was also moving up the hallway.

It turned and saw Lee and Banjo, lowered its head and got ready ... to attack.

Chapter Eight
RAGING RAPTORS

Arbee was not having a good day. His ship had been invaded by a pack of some of the most vicious and smartest dinosaurs that ever lived, but what made things worse was that he had gone all the way to deck one and had not found any of them.

"Frustrating, very frustrating," he thought. He called Zinzu. "Zinzu, what is your situation on the bridge?"

Zinzu replied, "We are alright here. One Deinonychus made it to the bridge, but I have neutralized it."

Then Sam cut in, "Arbee, there is something else."

"What is that?" asked Arbee.

"When the Raptor came to the bridge, it didn't attack me," she said.

"Oh? That is strange. Go on," said Arbee.

"Instead – and this is really weird – it went straight to the kitchen and ate all of your fried chicken," said Sam.

"Fried chicken, you say?" exclaimed Arbee. "Hmm, that is odd."

"I swear. It ate the fried chicken," said Sam. "That's the second time, too, remember ... back in the clearing? Scarface ate a piece of fried chicken that Banjo dropped."

"Well, I thought my cooking was good, but ..." said Arbee.

"I think there is something in the chicken they are after," said Sam. "Didn't you say it had lots of vitamins and stuff in it?"

"Yes, it is, but I find it hard to believe. All this for fried chicken?" asked Arbee. "Then again, there may be something to your theory."

Zinzu interrupted the conversation.

"Arbee, my scans show that Banjo and Lee are surrounded by Raptors!" he exclaimed.

"Which deck?" asked Arbee.

"Between decks three and four," said Zinzu.

"On my way," yelled Arbee. He flew down to the elevator on deck two. He pushed some buttons that cancelled the stop-elevator-command that was caused by the alarm going off.

The elevator would have him to deck three in just a few seconds – SWOOSH – the door opened and – SWOOSH – it closed. Arbee was on his way to rescue his friends.

"I hope I am not too late," he said. "What a day!"

If Arbee thought he was having a bad day, he should have seen the day poor Lee and Banjo were having.

They had barely escaped a Raptor attack in the elevator on deck one, climbed all the way up the inside of the ship to deck two, only to be attacked again by another Raptor. They climbed through the ship once more and made it to deck three. It looked safe, so they got out and ran towards the bridge on deck five. But just before they got to deck four, they practically tripped over the same Raptor from deck two.

Things were about to get a lot worse ...

"AAAAH," yelled Lee. "Go back, go back!"

The boys turned and ran, but when they rounded the corner going in the other direction, they looked down the deck three hallway and saw Scarface and his mate running straight for them.

"Oh man!" yelled Lee. "These things are everywhere. We are trapped!"

"Follow me," yelled Banjo, "and get your slingshot ready!"

They ran back up the hallway towards deck four.

"But Banjo, there is a Raptor up here!" yelled Lee.

"We will have to blast him!" yelled Banjo. "Fighting one is better than fighting two of those things. Come on, run!"

They turned the corner and there, only fifteen feet away, was the waiting Deinonychus.

"FIRE!" yelled Banjo.

THWACK, THWACK – The boys fired. The two flash marbles hit their target, but, instead of exploding in a flash of light and putting the dinosaur to sleep, the marbles hit the Deinonychus – THUD – and just FELL TO THE FLOOR but, they did not FLASH.

The Raptor was confused at first, but then became even angrier than before. It growled and moved closer. The boys were stunned.

"What happened?" yelled Lee. "Those things always work. We have used them a hundred times before!"

"They must be duds," yelled Banjo. "Reload, hurry!"

The boys each grabbed another marble and – THWACK, THWACK – fired again – PLOP, PLOP – they both hit the Raptor and bounced off the Deinonychus. It flinched and hissed a warning at the boys, but still NO FLASH.

"THEY ARE ALL DUDS!" yelled Lee.

The boys heard growling behind them. They looked over their shoulders and screamed.

Back on the bridge, Sam and Zinzu were anxiously watching their sensors.

"Oh, no," whispered Sam. "Lee and Banjo are trapped, Zinzu. We have got to do something."

"We must stay here," said Zinzu. "If the dinosaurs get to the bridge they could damage it causing us to be trapped in this time and die. Arbee is on his way. He will get to them on time I am sure of it."

All this time, Dino had been sitting by the entrance of the door, guarding with Bootsey. Suddenly, his dog ears heard a faint sound. Was it ...? Yes, it was Banjo and he was screaming.

He turned to Bootsey. "I have got to go protect Banjo ... he is in trouble. Can you guard this place?" thought Dino.

"No problem," thought Bootsey, "if they come in here, I'll scratch their eyes out ... GO."

Dino took off running as fast as his legs would go. He went down the ramp from deck five to deck four. He got to the hallway on deck four and kept running, puff, huff, puff. "This ship is too big," he thought.

Puff, huff, huff, he rounded another corner and at the far end of the passageway, he saw Lee and Banjo backed into a corner, shooting dud marbles at two very irritated and very angry Raptors. Dino charged straight for them, like a big furry cannon ball.

Arbee had arrived on deck three. The door opened and he flew out, but just as he did – WHAM – he smashed into a speeding Deinonychus. It was Scarface's mate. She was so stunned by the collision that she fell to the ground, but she recovered quickly, getting back to her feet. She growled and charged Arbee, while Scarface continued after Lee and Banjo.

Arbee had been smashed into a wall and was a little

stunned himself. His electronic body was tough, but he had just been hit by a one-hundred and seventy-five pound dinosaur, running as fast as it could go, and that was rough treatment even for him.

The Raptor leaped into the air straight at Arbee. Arbee dodged her, but one of the claws on her foot hit him and sent Arbee spinning into another wall.

She recovered and charged again. Once again Arbee zipped out of the way of the growling female and her claws missed him by inches. She turned again. Arbee flew down the hallway to put some distance between him and the beast.

"Do you Raptors ever get tired?" he asked.

"Rerrrraaaw," she replied.

"Apparently not," mumbled Arbee.

She crouched low to the ground and took off running straight at Arbee. But Arbee was ready this time. The Deinonychus leaped into the air, her deadly foot claws aimed straight for Arbee's head.

Arbee swooped to the ground, underneath the flying Raptor. He aimed his finger and fired – ZAP – a bolt of blue light shot out of his hand. The Deinonychus fell to the ground, knocked out, but she landed right on top of Arbee, pinning him to the floor.

"Blasted pest!" cursed Arbee. "Get ... off ... of ... me ... this ... instant ... Do you hear?"

Lee and Banjo thought they were dead meat for sure. They were pinned up against the wall, cornered by Scarface and the other Raptor, and were shooting the useless dud flash ball marbles at them and yelling at the beasts, trying to scare them away.

"GET AWAY! GET AWAY!" Lee yelled desperately.

The Raptors were standing there, taking their time. They would attack when they were ready. They knew these creatures were no match for them. They would let the strange creatures tire themselves out and then they would finish them off and get their food.

But what Scarface and the other Deinonychus did not see was an angry Chow Chow dog charging like an angry buffalo from behind. Dino got to the first Deinonychus. He leaped into the air and with all his seventy-eight pounds of weight – SLAM– smashed into the dinosaur's rib cage. The Raptor went down. Its feathers and fluff were flying everywhere. Dino had knocked the breath out of it and it lay on the ground gasping for air.

Scarface jumped back, startled by the sudden attack. "What is that thing?" he thought.

Dino, who recovered from his pounce, went straight for Scarface's stomach and bit him hard, sinking his sharp teeth into its thick, feathery hide.

"EEEERRK!" Scarface screamed, trying to back away

from Dino, but Dino hung on. Scarface swiped Dino with his sharp claws, but Dino held on.

The boys saw their chance.

"RUN," yelled Lee. "RUN NOW!"

Lee leaped over the first Raptor and ran. Then Banjo tried to jump over it but he tripped and fell right on top of the injured Deinonychus.

"EEEERROWW!" it screamed with pain.

It tried to bite and claw Banjo but he escaped and ran as fast as he could with Lee towards the bridge.

But Dino was still fighting for his life!

Chapter Nine
FINGER-LICKIN' GOOD CHICKEN

Lee and Banjo had escaped the Raptors and made it halfway down the hallway when Banjo stopped and yelled, "DINO, DROP THE DINOSAUR! DROP THE DINOSAUR, NOW, AND COME HERE! COME ON BOY!"

Dino did what Banjo told him to. He let go of Scarface and ran for Banjo.

"I am glad to be out of there," he thought. "That thing is MAD!" he thought.

"Uh oh, here comes Scarface ... AGAIN," yelled Lee.

"Let's get out of here!" yelled Banjo.

The three started running again, towards the bridge.

Scarface was angrier than ever. No one had ever challenged him and lived. He had taken on dinosaurs three times his size and won. He went after Lee, Banjo, and Dino more determined than ever.

The other Raptor was still trying to get its breath, but soon it too was back on its feet. Its ribs hurt badly and it was limping along at a much slower pace than Scarface, so Scarface left the injured Deinonychus behind.

Banjo, Lee, and Dino rounded the corner and were almost to deck five when Lee looked back over his shoulder.

"Banjo, Scarface is right behind us. He is going to catch us for sure!" yelled Lee. "We have got to do something."

"AAAAH, I am sick of being chased by these things," yelled Banjo. He stopped, took off his backpack, turned and ran right for Scarface.

Scarface stopped. What was this creature doing? Was it actually charging him? That was pretty desperate for sure.

"Banjo, NO!" yelled Lee. "What are you doing? STOP!"

Banjo was screaming like a crazy man and swinging his backpack over his head like it was a weapon. Banjo threw the pack as hard as he could right at the Raptor and – THWAP – he hit Scarface in the chest.

The pack fell to the floor. Scarface, who was stunned, stopped. Banjo just stood there staring at Scarface not sure what to do next.

Dino moved to Banjo's side and growled, preparing for another fight.

Lee had never seen Banjo so angry in his whole life.

"ARF, ARF, ARF!" Dino barked. "I took out your friend

and I'll take you out, too, bird-lizard!"

It was then that the strangest thing happened. Scarface just stood there looking at Banjo's pack. He did not attack Banjo, Dino, or Lee. Instead, he reached down and picked up Banjo's backpack. He easily tore it open with his sharp claws and out dropped all of Banjo's things, like his water, energy bars, computer, and a big container of Arbee's fried chicken.

Scarface grabbed the container of fried chicken and ripped it open and ...

"What is he doing?" whispered Lee.

"He is eating my fried chicken again!" said Banjo, as he and Dino backed slowly away. "What is up with this guy? Hey, dinosaur! You are eating chicken. That makes you a cannibal you know."

"I KNEW it," said a voice from behind the boys.

"AAAAH!" screamed the boys, who were frightened by the voice.

"SAM!" yelled Lee, "and Zinzu ... Man, am I glad to see you two. I hope you guys brought some kind of weapon with you, because we have got a major dinosaur problem."

"No weapons, no problem," said Sam. "Stand aside, boys."

Sam, walked right past Dino and the boys, followed by Zinzu. They were carrying two big bowls of fried chicken from Arbee's kitchen.

"Sam, get back here. Are you crazy?" yelled Lee. "Has everybody LOST THEIR MINDS TODAY?"

"Here Scarface, is this what you're looking for?" asked Sam.

Sam and Zinzu put the bowls down on the floor, making sure not to get too close to the Deinonychus. Scarface first sniffed then started eating the chicken in one of the bowls. He was soon joined by the other Raptor, who ate from the other bowl.

Banjo and Lee were shocked.

"You mean this whole thing was about fried chicken?" exclaimed Banjo. "That's it?"

"Do you remember in the clearing?" said Sam.

"You mean when I dropped the chicken?" said Banjo.

"Yes, when you dropped the chicken," said Sam, "and monster bird boy here ate it."

"So? So what?" said Banjo. "It's just chicken. These guys will probably eat anything."

"It is NOT just chicken," said a British-sounding voice that came from down the hallway.

"Arbee," said Sam. "Are you okay? You look scratched up!"

"Hello, everyone," replied Arbee. "Yes, I am fine. I have a few dents and dings in my body and I am in need of some minor repairs, but I will be fine."

Arbee floated past Scarface and his friend. They paid no attention to Arbee. They were too busy eating chicken.

"I proved my theory about the chicken," said Sam. "There is something in that stuff that attracts Raptors like bears to honey."

"Yes, Samantha, it seems you were right all along," admitted Arbee. "You see, when I created this food, I make it a complete food with lots of vitamins and minerals in it."

Life forms such as the Deinonychus here and even you are naturally attracted to foods that fill your body's needs," he explained. "That is why you have a sense of taste and smell and why you crave certain foods."

"So, you're a better cook than you thought," added Lee.

"Yes," Arbee sighed. "It seems my cooking is in great demand on your planet ... too much demand, I am afraid."

"May I suggest we cook up more of the chicken and use it to lead these dinosaurs out of the ship, before they do any more damage," said Zinzu.

"Yes, good idea," said Arbee. "But we should take them out another exit. No doubt there are more of these creatures hiding right outside the same door these creatures came in."

"There are at least three that I know of," said Sam. "I checked the computer sensors."

While the two Deinonychuses were still eating, Arbee and Zinzu, with the help of the Science Team, prepared more chicken.

Zinzu then carried a large platter of it right past the two Raptors, who were quite calm now. They followed Zinzu like dogs about to be fed, to the ship's back exit. When they were outside, Zinzu set the chicken on the ground.

"There you go Mr. Scarface," Zinzu said. "Now you are where you are supposed to be. Eat up and … stay … off … my … ship!"

While Zinzu was getting rid of Scarface and his friend Arbee had taken out something that looked like a thick floating tray. It made lifting beams of light so he could gently pick up the other two sleeping Raptors and carry them outside.

The Science Team brought out more platters of chicken.

Arbee woke up the sleeping Raptors. Then he used a medical tool that shot a beam of light, into the side of one of them. The beam healed the rib of the Deinonychus that had been attacked by Dino.

"Well, Dino, my boy," said Arbee, patting the Chow Chow on the head. "You certainly took care of that bird-lizard, I would say."

"GRRR, WOOF," barked Dino. "Bird-lizards should definitely not mess with Chow Chows," he thought.

"Right you are," agreed Arbee. "Do not mess with Chow Chow dogs."

The Science Team watched the Raptors eat their home-cooked meal from the safety of the starship's computer screens.

"ARK, ARK, ARK," Scarface called into the night for the other three Deinonychuses to come to dinner. The pack ate every scrap of chicken with the bones and everything. Then they licked their jaws, and slowly disappeared into the forest and back to their caves.

"Those are the best-fed dinosaurs that ever lived," said Sam.

"Well, I am glad they are GONE," said Lee. "Hey, Banjo, next time..."

"Next time what?" asked Banjo.

"Next time, don't feed the Raptors," said Lee.

They all laughed. It was the end of a very long and a very rough night.

"Back to the bridge, everyone," said Arbee. "I can fix you all something to eat, if you like," he added.

"No more fried chicken!" grumbled Banjo.

As they all went out back to the bridge, Lee remembered something. He reached into his pocket and pulled out some of the flash marbles Arbee had given the boys.

"Arbee, I don't know if you know this or not, but these flash marbles you gave us for our slingshots are all duds. They did not work," complained Lee.

Arbee stopped and thought for a moment. "No, they are not 'duds', as you call them," explained Arbee. "Those flash marbles will not work aboard this ship."

"Huh?" said Lee.

"That is because they not only knock out life forms," said Arbee, "they also can damage electrical circuits, such as power lines, computers, that sort of thing. So, I designed them so they would not blow up on the starship. I would hate to be stranded in this time with a wrecked ship."

"That would have been nice to know," grumbled Banjo, who was lagging behind the others.

When they got to the bridge, they all went into Arbee's kitchen to sit down and rest. Banjo stumbled in.

Arbee looked at Banjo as he walked in. "Banjo," he said, "are you sure you are all right?" Banjo looked pale and sickly.

"I don't really feel so good," mumbled Banjo. Suddenly, he swayed and fell to the ground, almost hitting Bootsey.

"BANJO!" yelled Lee.

Everyone ran to Banjo's side. Arbee sat him up and noticed the side of his shirt was wet.

"Oh no, that is blood," gasped Sam. "Banjo's hurt!"

Arbee lifted Banjo's shirt and saw a six-inch-long cut on Banjo's side.

"He must have got that when he fell on top of the Raptor in the hall," whispered Lee. "It looks bad."

Arbee felt Banjo's pulse. "Zinzu," he whispered, "help me get him to the Body-Repair room and quickly. He is very weak."

Chapter Ten
ARBEE CALLS 911

Arbee and Zinzu carried Banjo into the ship's Body-Repair room and laid him on a floating computerized medical table. They asked Lee and Sam to be very quiet while they ran some tests and scans on Banjo's body.

"The toxin from the Deinonychus has gotten into his blood stream," said Zinzu. "It is affecting his heart."

"Can we neutralize it?" asked Arbee.

"I will try," said Zinzu.

"Do what you can. Keep me informed," requested Arbee.

"Is Banjo okay?" asked Lee. "I mean, is he going to ..."

"Banjo's injury is serious," said Arbee. "I may have to do something extreme, but I will not let him die."

"What do you mean by 'do something extreme'?" asked Lee.

"Patience, Lee," said Arbee. "Zinzu is doing everything possible. All we can do is let him do his job."

"REEOWWW, REEOWWW!" Bootsey the cat was upset about something and was pawing at Sam's leg.

"Bootsey, not now," whispered Sam, as she pushed the cat away.

"REEOWWW!" Bootsey would not stop pawing at Sam.

"Okay," said Sam. "What?" She followed the anxious cat to the hallway just outside of the Body-Repair room. Sam saw Dino lying in the middle of the hall.

Bootsey ran up to Dino. "REEOWWW!" he cried. "Something's wrong with Dino," he thought. "He is hurt."

Sam ran over to Dino. "Oh no, ARBEE! COME QUICK!"

Arbee flew out of Body-Repair and over to where Dino was laying.

"Dino is hurt, too!" exclaimed Sam. "See?"

Arbee saw a red spot on Dino's left rear leg. Dino had so much hair that no one had noticed it before. Arbee moved Dino's fur and saw a deep cut about an inch or two long.

Dino whimpered a little from the pain. "Ouch! Easy, Arbee," he thought. "I don't feel so good ..."

"I am sorry, Dino," whispered Arbee. "Zinzu, we have another patient here," he called.

Soon they had another floating medical table set up and

carefully laid Dino on it.

Zinzu did some tests. "Well, Dino is doing better than Banjo. I will need some help in here. I have much work to do to try and get that toxin out of their bodies."

"I'll help," said Lee. "My uncle is a doctor and he lets me help him sometimes. Anyway, I want to help. Banjo is my friend, and I am not leaving him, or Dino."

Arbee and Zinzu were not going to argue with Lee.

"Very well," said Arbee. "If Zinzu has no objection ..."

Even before he had finished talking, Zinzu had put Lee to work handing him different alien medical tools.

"Samantha, you and I are needed on the bridge," said Arbee.

"Okay," said Sam. She was trying not to cry.

Arbee and Sam left the Body-Repair room and went back to the bridge.

Bootsey stayed with Dino. "He may be a dog but I like the big fur ball," he thought.

"Will they be all right?" asked Sam, as she stood at her computer control board.

"Yes, they will," said Arbee. "But it may mean we will have to leave this time and fly back to my home planet."

"You mean to Planet Izikzah?" asked Sam. "Well, that is kind of far. How long would that take?"

"Yes, to Planet Izikzah," answered Arbee as he was working, "and we could be there in less than forty-five minutes at super-light speed."

"But why?" asked Sam. "Isn't your medical equipment good enough on this ship?"

"No, this is a research vessel. We may not have the advanced Body-Repair tools needed to give Banjo and Dino the treatment they need," said Arbee. "I can send you and Lee home, if you would like, and then return Banjo and Dino when their bodies have been repaired."

"No way," said Sam. "I mean ... I want to go ... they are my friends. Please let me go. It's not against your laws is it, because we are from another planet?"

"No, Samantha, it is not against our laws," said Arbee. "And if you and Lee want to go, I could use the help."

"Good," she said, "then I will help you with whatever you need."

Just then, Zinzu called over the ship's radio. "Arbee, this is Zinzu here."

"Go ahead," said Arbee. "What is happening with Banjo and Dino?"

"Both patients are in stable condition, for now," replied Zinzu. "But for some unknown reason, their wounds will not heal. I recommend they be transported to a better equipped Body-Repair facility, immediately or they could die from blood loss."

"I understand," said Arbee. "Prepare the patients for takeoff. We are leaving for home planet at once. Lee, are you there?"

"Yeah, I am here," answered Lee.

"Lee, we must go to Planet Izikzah to save your friends. You can go with us or ..."

"I am staying with Dino and Banjo," interrupted Lee. "Just hurry up, please. Banjo doesn't look so good. He is really pale and I think he has a bad fever."

"I will hurry, Lee," replied Arbee. "Samantha, do you remember what I taught you about the steps for flying the starship off the ground? You are going to have to do some of Zinzu's job."

"Yes ... I think I remember," said Sam. She quickly punched a series of buttons on two computer boards. She felt better being busy, at least she was helping.

"Alright, here we go. Lift off in three ... two ... and ... time change," said Arbee.

The huge round starship shot into space and began to orbit the earth at unbelievable speed. Soon the stars and the earth were just a blur of different colored lights. It made Sam a little dizzy to watch on the ship's main viewing screen.

"Approaching present time," said Arbee. "Leaving orbit in three ...two ... one ... NOW!

WOOSH – the starship flew away from earth and its solar system so fast it was like a lightning flash. Sam grabbed

99

her computer board expecting to be splattered against the back wall of the ship, but nothing happened at all.

"Do not worry," assured Arbee. "The ship's gravity computers make it so we have a very smooth ride."

"Phew, that's good!" she gasped. Sam was dizzy from the time change, but she shook her head kept working at her computer.

Arbee pushed some buttons on his computer that showed the view of space as they left Earth's star system.

"Do you see that tiny star?" asked Arbee.

"Yes," said Sam. "That's not Earth's sun, is it?"

"It most certainly is," said Arbee.

"Whoa, we are going fast!" exclaimed Sam. "Hey, Arbee, I can't see the stars! They are just faint steaks of light!"

"That happens when you travel faster than light," said Arbee. "Do not worry. I assure the stars are still there."

"Oh ... did you know that our scientists on earth say that you can't travel faster than light," said Sam. "Some guy named Einstein made a law against it."

"Well ... I will not tell Mr. Einstein if you will not tell him either," laughed Arbee.

Sam laughed, "That's okay ... I think the guy is dead, anyways."

Back in the Body-Repair room, Zinzu finished his work.

"Well, Lee, we have done what we can do for now," whispered Zinzu. "Thank you for your help."

"Okay," replied Lee. "How come you are whispering?"

"Oh, our body-engineers, or doctors, as you call them, have learned never to make noise around a life form that is unconscious."

"But, why?" asked Lee.

"Because the mind records everything, even when you are unconscious," said Zinzu, "and those memories can cause problems later on."

Lee remembered a time when he was sick when he was younger. The people around him made a lot of noise and he remembered it bothered him so he kept his voice down. "I just hope they get better," he sighed.

It was not long before the starship began to slow down. Sam could feel it. "Are we almost there?" she asked.

"Yes, we will be coming out of super-light speed in three … two … one … NOW!"

The starship trembled as it slowed down to a normal speed. Sam could see on the view screen what were just

streaks of light become stars again. In another few seconds, a large bluish-green planet came into view.

"Is that your planet?" whispered Sam.

"Yes that is the planet Izikzah," answered Arbee. "It is the main planet in a system of three livable planets. It is bigger than Earth, but has similar atmosphere so you will have no trouble breathing. You will feel a little heavier, though."

Arbee pushed a computer button. "Zinzu, come in."

"Zinzu here," he replied.

"We are approaching home planet. How are the patients?" asked Arbee.

"They are alive," replied Zinzu, "but they are losing blood and they are getting weaker. We must get them to Body-Repair quickly or they will not last much longer."

"I understand. Please prepare Dino and Banjo for arrival," said Arbee, "and give Lee a translator badge."

"Will do. Zinzu out."

Arbee reached into a compartment under the control board and pulled out a button-sized badge.

"Here, Samantha, put this on," said Arbee.

"What is it?" she asked, as she clipped it to her shirt.

"It is a translator badge," answered Arbee. "We do not speak the same language as you do, but this badge will make it sound like we do. And it translates your language into ours, so you will be understood."

"Wow, okay," Sam said.

"Samantha, push that blue button on your control board, please," said Arbee.

Sam pushed the button and Arbee spoke.

"This is Research Vessel 220 to Section Six, Traffic Control. Come in, please."

"This is traffic control, Section Six. Go ahead RV 220," a voice on the speakers said. "What is your situation please?"

"I am declaring a class one medical emergency," said Arbee, "and request immediate clearance to the Section Six Body-Engineering facility."

"Message received, RV 220," said the voice. "Please stand by."

A few seconds went by and …

"RV 220, you are authorized for immediate landing at Bio-engineering facility, Section Six. Change your course to seventy-two point five."

"Changing course to seventy-two point five," said Arbee. "Thank you, Traffic Control. RV 220 out."

"Good luck, RV 220. Sector Six, Traffic Control out," said the voice.

Arbee then made a call to an old friend. Sam could

see on Arbee's computer screen a robot that looked a little like Zinzu, except it had four eyes and four arms, and it was different colors.

"This is Arbee, is Bers there? It is urgent ... a class one medical emergency," said Arbee.

"Yes, he is in," replied the operator. "Please hold while I connect you."

"Thank you," said Arbee.

In a matter of seconds, another floating alien came on the screen. Sam could see this one had a tall oval-shaped body with two eyes and four arms. Its body was more complicated than Arbee's.

"Well, Arbee, I have not seen you in an age!" said the alien Bers.

"It has been a while," said Arbee. "We need to catch up. But, I have an emergency and I need your help."

"An emergency in the library research department?" said Bers. "You people have the peaceful jobs, from what I hear."

"Do not believe a word of it," said Arbee. "Some of the life forms we encounter back in time are extremely dangerous."

"You will have to tell me about it later," said Bers. "I would be glad to help you in any way I can. What is the emergency?"

"I have a team of science ambassadors from Planet

Earth that have been assisting me," explained Arbee, "and two of them are seriously injured and in need of advanced Body-Repair."

"Planet Earth ... I have never heard of Planet Earth," he replied. "Are we in contact with this planet?" he asked.

"Not officially," replied Arbee.

"I see," said Bers. "Well, never mind. What body types are we dealing with?"

"One two-legged human and one four-legged canine or dog body," said Arbee.

"Hmmm ... human and canine, so they are flesh bodies," said Bers. "Right, bring them at once to Bio-Repair, Section Six, dock Seventeen at once. I will meet you there with my team."

"Your help is greatly appreciated," said Arbee.

"Do not thank me yet, old friend," he warned, "until I am sure I can help your people. Flesh bodies such as theirs are very fragile. Let us hope they have not busted them up too badly. Oh and please make sure Zinzu gives me the body-data-disk on both patients, Bers out."

"We will have all the data you need. Arbee out."

"Flesh bodies are very fragile," Sam thought. "I don't like the sound of that ... at all."

Chapter Eleven
ALIEN OPERATION

Arbee, Zinzu, Lee, and Sam loaded Banjo and Dino, on their floating medical tables, aboard a shuttle craft that looked like a large bug. Arbee and Sam flew the shuttle out of the starship that was parked in the sky, next to some other starships, above the planet's surface.

As they flew down to the surface, Sam, Lee and Bootsey were looking out the ship's windows at another world, the planet Izikzah.

Izikzah was a beautiful planet covered with large forests of different color trees and plants. There were trees that were blue others were red, yellow, and orange. It looked like a painting. In between the large colorful forests of trees, were groups of colorful buildings. They were all different sizes of dome shapes.

"Boy, these aliens sure like color," thought Sam. "It looks like somebody spilled paints all over the place."

Planet Izikzah was busy. There were spaceships, aliens, and shuttle craft zooming everywhere. It was a beehive of activity.

"Wow! Lee, think of it, we are the first Earth people to visit an alien planet," whispered Sam. "Isn't this the coolest thing ever?"

"Yeah, I guess," sighed Lee. He was not paying much attention to the sights. He was worried about his injured friend Banjo and Dino as well.

Sam patted Lee on the shoulder. "Don't worry. If anybody can save Banjo and Dino, these guys can, I know it."

Sam really did not know whether or not they could be saved for sure, she just wanted to cheer Lee up.

"Arbee." said Lee.

"Yes, Lee," said Arbee as he flew the shuttle craft.

"So, who is this Bers guy?" asked Lee. "Is he a doctor or something?"

"Yes, and much more," said Arbee. "As I told you earlier, we do not use names on our planet, so BERS stands for Body Engineer, Repair Specialist or what you would call ... a doctor. He is one of the best in his field at repairing bodies. Hold on, we are about to land."

The shuttle flew into the opening at the bottom of a large green dome-shaped building and landed inside. There were three floating aliens, along with Bers waiting nearby.

"Alright, everybody, please help me push the floating medical tables out of the shuttle craft," whispered Arbee.

Lee and Zinzu pushed Banjo's table out, while Arbee and Sam, with Bootsey close behind, pushed Dino's table out.

They were greeted by Bers. "Hello, everyone, welcome to Planet Izikzah," he said quietly.

Arbee introduced everyone to his old friend, but they kept the greetings short, because Bers was concerned about the two patients, Banjo and Dino.

"Zinzu, let me have their body-data disks, please," said Bers.

"I have them here as you requested," said Zinzu, and he handed a small gold disk to Bers.

Bers inserted the disk into a slot in his chest and looked at it. "Hmmm, interesting," he mumbled. "Well, I take back what I said, Arbee. A library researcher's job is a great deal more dangerous than I ever imagined. Tell me, do you have a sample of this Deinonychus poison with you?"

"No, because the injury occurred in a past time," said Arbee, "but we do have a chemical break down. Samantha, do you have the disk?"

"Yes ... right here," said Sam. She handed the second disk to Bers.

"Good," said Bers. "Let's move the patients to Body-Repair Room forty-three, at once," he told his assistants.

Bers and his assistants pushed the floating medical tables quickly across the landing area and down a long hallway. As they walked, Lee got up enough courage to talk to Bers.

"So, can I call you doctor?" asked Lee. "That is what we call body-repair guys on my planet."

Bers looked at him. "Yes, doctor will be fine," he said.

"Okay," said Lee. "So, how are you going to fix Banjo's body? What I mean is, he is a human and you're, well ... you are different."

Bers laughed quietly.

"What's so funny?" asked Lee.

"Tell me, Lee," said Bers, "how much do you know about life and civilizations in this galaxy?"

"Nothing," mumbled Lee. "We didn't even know about your people until we met Arbee by accident. On my planet, if you believe in aliens or space ships, people will think you are some kind of a kook and they won't talk to you."

"Earth does not have space travel except around their planet," added Arbee.

"Ahhh, I see," said Bers. "Well, it might interest you to know that human bodies like yours have been in use in different parts of this galaxy for billions of years. So, I know exactly how they work and how to fix them. Some of the inside organs are a little different from planet to planet, but I have repaired them all. I am skilled in repairing over five thousand different body types, including humans and dogs like your friends here."

"That's the best news I have heard all day," said Lee quietly.

"Here we are, Body Repair Room forty-three," said Bers.

Banjo and Dino, still sleeping quietly, were pushed into an empty room with a large computer at one end.

"Can I stay and help?" asked Lee. "I won't get in the way, I promise. Please?"

Bers thought for a moment. "Very well," he said, "but you will need to be sterilized and put on some protective robes and a mask."

"Okay," said Lee, "I will do it."

One of the assistant aliens floated over to Lee and sprayed him with a beam of light. Then the assistant went to a wall, opened a hidden door and produced a green robe, hat, and mask. Lee put them on. They were a strange shape and a little big on him, so he rolled up his sleeves to make it fit. They were made for an alien body.

"The rest of you, please stand on the far side of the room," said Bers. Then he told one of the assistants, "Turn on the clean-screen."

"The clean-screen is on," said the assistant. A see through electronic screen went on separating the others from Bers, his assistants, Lee, and the patients.

"So that's to keep germs out, right, doctor?" asked Lee.

"Correct," said Bers. "The medical tables that your friends are on have a protective screen around them, too, so I must turn it off so I can do my work on them. This room must be protected from germs, first."

"Please turn the table screens off," ordered Bers.

The assistants floated over and pushed a button on the side of the floating tables. "Table screens are off," said the assistants.

"Now, let me have a look here," whispered Bers.

He looked at a computer at the end of the floating table. It showed all of Banjo's insides, including his heart and other organs. Then he did the same to Dino. He pushed a lot of buttons on both tables and studied the computer information carefully. Lee was watching everything very closely.

"Banjo has a fever, I think," said Lee. "See, he is sweating."

"You are right," whispered Bers. "It is from the dinosaur toxin. His body is trying to fight it. This is very bad stuff."

"Are you going to give him drugs or antibiotics?" Lee asked.

"No," said Bers. "We have to get the poison out of their bodies first and then get the cells to heal themselves. Drugs slow the healing. Our medicine advanced past the need for drugs many thousands of years ago."

"And antibiotics kill only certain types of germs," Bers added. "This is a poison, not a germ so they will not work for this."

"But, aren't they in pain without a pain drug?" asked Lee.

"No, they are not," said Bers. "We get rid of the pain with electronic screens and there are no after effects. Drugs have dangerous side effects. Most civilizations have not used them for centuries. And as I said, they are a very ancient form of medicine."

"Oh," said Lee.

"Ah, ha, I have found it," whispered Bers.

"What have you found?" asked Arbee.

"These Deinonychus beasts have a very interesting poison in their saliva and in their claws," explained Bers. "What this poison does is it keeps cuts, scrapes, and wounds from healing. You see?"

"When they hunt down an animal and slash it with their teeth and claws, if the animal doesn't die and runs away, its wounds will not heal," he explained. "That way the creatures can track it down until they can kill it or ... it bleeds to death. That is why even after treatment the patients still would not get better. I have seen this poison before, but it is rare."

"So, what do we do now?" asked Lee.

Bers had his assistants get two sphere-shaped objects, the size of a baseball. They handed them to the alien doctor.

Bers pushed some buttons on each sphere.

"Lee, you can help," he said. "Take this sphere and hold it over Dino's body and do exactly what I do."

Bers held his sphere over Banjo. Lee did the same over Dino.

"Push the blue button," said Bers, "and slowly move it over Dino's whole body, from head to toe. Go ahead, just do like I do."

"Okay, I pushed the button," said Lee, "and I am moving it over Dino's body like you said."

"Alright, keep doing it slowly. Make sure you go over every part of the body," said Bers. "We want to cover all the blood vessels and the organs — like the heart, liver and kidneys — because that is where the poison is."

"I think I got it," said Lee. "Hey, doctor, Dino's heart is getting stronger. I can see it on the computer screen."

"Good," said Bers. "That is what we want it to do. Keep it up. It is working."

"What's it doing?" asked Sam.

"We are turning the poison in their bodies into a harmless liquid that their bodies can absorb," said Bers. "By getting rid of the toxins, our patient's bodies can be repaired."

After about twenty minutes, a red light on each of the spheres turned green.

"That means the poison is gone," said Bers. "You can

stop now and hand the sphere to the assistant."

Lee gave the sphere to the assistant, who turned it off, cleaned it and put it away.

Bers asked his assistant, "I need a C.G. Wand, please.

"What is a C.G. Wand?" asked Lee

"C.G. stands for 'Cell Growth'," answered Bers. "Your body is made up of cells and this wand makes the cells grow faster. It heals wounds in just a few seconds. You can watch, if you like."

Bers took the strange looking wand from his assistant. He pushed some buttons on it. He lifted up Banjo's shirt and an assistant removed the bandage that Zinzu had put on the deep gash.

"Oh, that looks bad, poor Banjo," whispered Sam. She could not look and closed her eyes.

But Lee watched what Bers was doing with great interest. The doctor took the wand, pushed another button on it and waved it slowly over Banjo's wound. A bright green light came out of the end and shone on Banjo's side.

"Ohhh!" gasped Lee. "The cut, it is healing. It's like magic! Sam, you have got to see this. It is really working!"

The cut on Banjo's side was disappearing and soon Lee could not even tell where the injury had been. There was not even a scar. The Body-Repair assistants came over and cleaned up the blood off of Banjo's side.

"Unbelievable," whispered Sam. She was very relieved.

"What about Dino?" thought Bootsey. "Make them fix Dino, Arbee."

"Do not worry, Bootsey," said Arbee, as he scratched the cat's head. "Dino is next."

When he was finished with Banjo, Bers floated over to Dino and healed his wound with the C. G. Wand. Then the assistants cleaned up Dino as well.

"All right, everyone, good job. Go ahead and wake them up now," whispered Bers to his assistants.

The assistants went to the far end of each table, pushed two buttons, and ...

"Ohhh, what the heck happened? Where am I anyway?" said Banjo. He looked over at Lee. "Hey ... what's with the weird doctor costume you're wearing?" he asked. "It's not Halloween, is it? Was I asleep for that long?"

" Doctor Bers and I just saved your life," answered Lee, who was smiling now.

"Doctor, what doctor?" Banjo sat up and looked at Bers.

"Hello, Banjo, welcome to Planet Izikzah," said Bers. "How do you feel now?"

"I feel good, now," said Banjo, "but, how did I get here?"

"I will let your friends explain," answered Bers.

"Woof, woof!" Dino was sitting up wagging his tail

"What is going on," he thought, "and who are all these Arbee-looking people?"

"I'll explain later," thought Bootsey." I am glad you are back in the world of the living, dog."

"Alright, please turn off the clean field," said Bers. "Arbee, I would like to do a body test of all the ambassadors from Earth, if that is all right with them."

"I have no objection, if they do not," said Arbee.

"Yeah, I'll do it," said Sam.

"Me, too," said Lee.

"Well ..." mumbled Banjo.

"Just do it, Banjo," said Lee. "These guys are cool, trust me. They totally saved your life just now."

"Well, okay," replied Banjo. "But, somebody needs to tell me what's going on."

While Bers did the medical test on Banjo, Lee, Sam, Dino, and Bootsey, Sam told Banjo what happened after he passed out on the starship's bridge and how they had to take him to the alien hospital.

Banjo turned to Arbee and Bers, "Thanks for saving me. I must have got cut when I tried to jump over the Deinonychus and fell on it. I was so excited that I didn't even feel it."

"You are very welcome," said Bers. "I enjoy making people well."

An assistant showed Bers the results of the medical scans on the Science Team. The doctor frowned. "Hmmm, interesting," he said.

"What? What's that?" said Lee. "Is there something wrong?"

"You are all showing signs of long-term poor nutrition and early body problems," said Bers.

"What do you mean by poor nutrition and body problems?" asked Lee

"It means the food you are eating is not good enough to run your bodies and they are slowly breaking down before they are supposed to," answered Bers.

"He means we are eating too much garbage and not enough good food," said Sam.

"Lee, the food you are getting seems to be better than your friends', here. What do you normally eat?" asked Bers.

"Well, my family is Chinese, so we eat a lot of rice, vegetables, and fish ... stuff like that," Lee said. "You know ... healthy stuff."

"I see," said Bers. "Arbee, there has to be something wrong with Planet Earth's food supply for something like this to occur I would expect these test results from one person but

119

not all of them."

"Yes, I suspected that, too," said Arbee. "I was having Zinzu investigate it, but then this happened."

Zinzu floated over. "I was able to do some checking on the history of planet Earth's food supply before the attack on our ship."

"And what did you find out?" asked Bers.

"My research was cut short but what I found out was that the people on Earth over process their food so much that they take most of the vitamins and minerals out of it. Then they add chemicals to the food to keep it from becoming rotten," said Zinzu.

"I do not understand. Why would they over process the food supply?" asked Bers.

"From what I could uncover, it was a solution to solve huge food shortage problems around the planet. By doing that to the food and adding chemicals, it makes the food last longer," said Zinzu.

"But the amount of disease on Earth is very high and poor food quality is one of the main reasons for this, so the 'solution' has become a bigger problem. And they have not solved this problem," added Zinzu

"I see," said BERS. "Well, I cannot help your whole planet, but, I can help you."

Bers asked his assistants for a cell-growth wand and a container full of some green tablets. He gave each of them a tablet, including Dino and Bootsey.

"Go on, chew them up," said Bers. "They will not hurt you, and they should taste good."

Sam was the first to take one. "Mmm, this tastes like chocolate," she said.

"Mine tastes like a cheeseburger," laughed Lee. "It's good."

"This one tastes like potato chips," said Banjo.

Bootsey's tasted like fish to him, and Dino's tasted like steak. "These alien guys always have the best food," thought Dino.

"I agree," thought Bootsey.

Then Bers waved the wand up and down each of their bodies for about a minute each.

"There," he said at last. "How do you feel?"

"I feel … great!" said Banjo. "I love alien science, it's awesome."

"Me, too," said Sam

"Yeah, I have never felt better" said Lee. "What did you do?"

"I pronounce you all cured and I release you from my care," said Bers. "But when you get back to Earth, I order you to eat better food, good food, not 'processed' or 'junk food', as you call it. You do not have to go on any strange or weird diets, just eat food in its natural state, and chew it well. Do not gulp it, understand?"

They all agreed.

One of Bers' assistants floated up to him. "You are needed in Section Five. We have another Body-Repair emergency. There has been an explosion aboard a Tharan Starship with many serious injuries."

"I see," said Bers. "Call as many of our Body-Repair people as you can and have them assemble at dock twenty-two."

"Right away," answered the assistant and flew off in an instant to another part of the hospital.

"It was a pleasure to meet you all, but as you see, I am needed somewhere else," said Bers. He turned to Arbee. "Good to see you again, old friend. Stay in touch."

"Thank you again," said Arbee. "I will."

Bers and his assistants flew out of the room to their next emergency.

"Hey, Arbee, do you think if I sent Bers an e-mail or a message that he will write me back?" asked Lee.

"Of course," said Arbee. "You can send a message from the starship, if you would like."

"Cool," sighed Lee. "Some day, I want to be a doctor like him," he thought, "and heal people."

"Now that I have seen your planet, how would you all like a tour of my planet, planet Izikzah?" asked Arbee.

Chapter Twelve

WE ARE LATE, WE ARE LATE, FOR A VERY IMPORTANT DATE!

The Science Team was now fully healed and felt better than ever. They loaded everything, including themselves, back aboard the bug shaped shuttle craft and took off.

"We need to load these medical tables back on board the starship," said Arbee. "But before that I need to make a quick stop at the Department of Ship Security, first."

"Why?" asked Sam. "You're not in any trouble, are you?"

"No, no," said Arbee. "They received my report about the attack on the starship and want to talk to us about it."

But Sam thought, "We are in trouble for sure."

Arbee and Zinzu flew the shuttle to another building about five miles from the Body-Repair hospital. This tall dome-shaped building was a bright yellow color.

"Boy, your people sure like color, don't they?" said Banjo, who was getting his first look at Planet Izikzah.

"I noticed that, too," laughed Sam.

"Yes, I suppose we do," laughed Arbee. "Hold on, we are landing now."

The shuttle flew into the entrance and parked. They were met by a tall, string-bean-looking alien with four arms. Arbee introduced the alien as SPIDO. That stood for Security, Protection, Intelligence, and Detection Officer.

"Greetings," said Spido. "Come into my office. I have received the security tapes of the attack on your starship by the Deinonychus creatures from your research in solar system 17552-3 and I have come up with a solution for you."

"How did you get the tapes so fast?" asked Sam.

"Oh ... the second-in-command of the starship RV-220, Officer Zinzu, sent them to me. When any ship of ours is attacked by anything or anyone, the tapes of the attack, if they are available, must immediately be sent to my section to be looked at," answered Spido.

"Wow, you guys are quick," said Sam. "We are in so much trouble," she mumbled shaking her head.

"Not quick enough, I am afraid," said Spido. "Security aboard library research vessels has started to become a bigger problem. You never know what sort of deadly life forms are running around on other planets, especially in the past."

The attack on RV 220 – which is research vessel 220,

your ship — was just the latest. But you are in luck, because from now on every research vessel ... all ten thousand one hundred forty-two of them ... will be supplied with these." Spido pulled out a container and opened it. Everyone looked in. In the box there were about ten glass-like spheres. They were red and were a little bigger than a baseball.

"Excellent," gasped Arbee. "I did not think the library research department would ever get these."

"It was just approved," said Spido happily. "My security team is delivering them to your starship as we speak!"

"What are they?" asked Lee, as he picked one up and looked it over.

"They look like glass baseballs to me," said Banjo.

"Protecto-Pods," said Spido. "With these fellows on the job, not even an insect will be able to sneak on board your ship. The instructions on how to use them will be on a disk in the package. Just insert the disk into your starship's computer, start them up and you will be as safe as a clam in a thick steel shell."

"That's a great idea!" said Lee. "We could use some more security. "I can't tell you how many times I have almost been eaten. If I get eaten, my mom will freak out."

"Thank you, Spido," said Arbee. "This will save lives."

"Think nothing of it," said Spido. "It was good to meet you all. Say hello to Planet Earth for me when you return. Oh, wait ... on second thought, maybe it is better that you do not do that. I understand the local authorities do not like aliens poking around in their business. Ha, ha, ha! Oh well, I must run along. There is a lot to do. Good bye and good spacing to you." He flew out of his office and disappeared down a long hallway.

"Phew," said Sam. "I thought we were in trouble for sure. On Earth if you mess up like that, then you can say goodbye to your job."

"Really?" asked Arbee.

"Really," said Sam. "My mom got fired once for losing some important papers!"

"I can see that if it was done on purpose," said Arbee, "but, if it was a mistake, you fix it and move on. Speaking of moving on, we must go. Everyone aboard the shuttle craft."

First they stopped off and unloaded the medical beds back onto the starship. While they were there they saw lots of aliens on the ship. They were carrying strange looking tools and parts and machines.

"Who are all these guys?" asked Lee. "They look like they are tearing your ship apart."

"Those are starship engineers and repair crews," explained Arbee. "They are fixing the damage that the dinosaurs did to the ship. When a ship is damaged the ship is not allowed to be flown until it is fixed."

"You cannot fly in space with a broken starship," added Zinzu. "Arbee, I will stay aboard and oversee the repairs."

"Alright, we will be back soon," he replied.

Then Arbee took the Science Team out for a look at his home world. They flew over large colorful cities of domed buildings. But planet Izikzah's cities were not all bunched together like Earth cities. They were spread out with forests of colorful trees in between groups of buildings.

"Hey Arbee, how come there aren't any roads between the buildings?" asked Lee.

"We do not need roads," said Arbee, "because our bodies, vehicles, and ships all fly."

"Are there any animals in those forests down there?" asked Banjo.

"Some squirrels would be nice," thought Dino. "But no dinosaur squirrels. That would be bad."

"Yes, there are animals," said Arbee. "I will fly lower so you can have a look. We have a wide variety of creatures that live on the land and in our oceans."

Arbee flew the shuttle down until it was almost touching the treetops.

"Ohhh, look at those pretty birds!" said Sam.

Bootsey noticed them, too. "Mmmm, birds, yum," he thought. "They look delicious."

A flock of bright blue and yellow birds with long streaming tails flew across the sky.

"Those are called Skeelots," said Arbee.

"Woof," Dino barked. "Got any rabbits?" he thought.

"Sorry, Dino, no rabbits," answered Arbee, "and there are not any squirrels for you, either."

The shuttle craft flew over a clearing where they saw a herd of animals. They had reddish brown hair with dull yellow spots. They looked like deer with strange ears and they were running and leaping through tall grasses.

In the trees were some dark orange animals with blue spots that looked like big possums. They were eating some sort of berries that grew in bunches under the leaves.

"Oooo, I could chase them!" thought Dino.

"They are probably poisonous," thought Bootsey. "Besides, haven't you chased enough stuff today?"

"Those are called Ogwans," said Arbee. "And yes, Bootsey and Dino, their bite is poisonous so we will not be chasing them today."

After the forest, they flew over a bright turquoise ocean where the water was so clear, you could see one hundred feet down. It was full of thousands of fish of every shape and size.

"Look at the size of those fish!" said Lee. "What are those called?"

"That is a school of Kootamahs," said Arbee. "They are similar to the whales on Earth, except they have four big fins like those sea dinosaurs ..."

"Like Elasmosaurs, or Plesiosaurs," interrupted Banjo.

"Exactly," said Arbee.

The Science Team watched the Kootamahs swim slowly along, through massive schools of colorful fish.

Arbee piloted the shuttle away from the ocean towards one of Planet Izikzah's many spaceports. As they approached, they could see how big the port was. It was similar to an airport, but much, much larger, with space ships of every size and shape taking off and landing.

"As I have told you, Planet Izikzah is a center for learning and its people are librarians and teachers," said Arbee.

"People from all over this part of the galaxy come to Izikzah to get advanced education and to do research in the Galactic Central Library. You can learn anything on any subject here," he said.

Arbee flew the shuttle craft to the planet's gigantic main spaceport. It was so busy with ships and vehicles flying everywhere that it looked like an alien beehive.

Dino and Bootsey were watching everything flying by.

"So many – it's like a bunch of alien bees," Dino thought.

"Look how busy this place is," said Lee. "How do you guys keep from running into each other?"

"This is no place to be day dreaming while you are flying a ship," said Arbee, "There are ships coming from thousands of different planets but we rarely have any crashes here. We have excellent air traffic controllers."

"You mean there is really life on that many planets?" asked Banjo.

"Yes," said Arbee. "Remember, Earth is on the edge of the galaxy. It is similar to living in the middle of a desert where you are. We will land and you can look for yourselves."

Arbee landed the shuttle in what looked like a huge parking lot. The Science Team took a flying bus quite some way to the main space port.

They walked into a clear glass dome building as big as a city. There were aliens everywhere. There were thousands of Arbee's people of every size, shape, and color floating by. Banjo noticed that very few of his people looked alike.

"Arbee, how come none of your people look the same?" asked Banjo.

"Well, what fun would that be?" asked Arbee, "Everyone looking the same is boring. We like looking different."

"Look," whispered Sam, "over there. I can't believe it!" She pointed to a group of tall, muscular men wearing blue uniforms. They looked like military officers.

"Awesome," whispered Banjo. "They are humans just like us!"

Banjo and Sam waved at them and they smiled and waved back.

"Bers said that there were humans all over the galaxy," said Lee.

"Yes, human-type bodies are quite common," said Arbee. "Those men are probably space fleet officers from the United Planets of the Mestoney. It is an empire of thirty-two worlds."

They saw another group of very tall human-like people with big, bald heads and pointed ears.

"That is a group of students from Planet Agas," whispered Arbee.

"Where are those guys from?" whispered Lee. He pointed to a group of men who had green lizard-like skin and lizard-like faces as well. "They are kind of scary looking."

"They are from the Distancian Empire," said Arbee. As a matter of fact, they are descendents from a dinosaur-type race of people."

"Really, dinosaur people?" whispered Banjo.

"Glad I don't live where they do," thought Dino.

"Me, too," thought Bootsey. "They would probably eat us, because they are lizard people."

They saw a woman walking several dogs through the space port.

"Hey, look over there … DOGS," thought Dino. Arbee, there are alien dogs!"

"Yes Dino and Bootsey there are even dogs and cats on other planets, too," Arbee said.

"I am not surprised that there are alien cats," thought Bootsey. "Cats are very smart, much smarter than people."

They saw many different-looking people, but Lee was surprised that there were no monster-looking aliens like in Hollywood movies. Most of them were just people with two arms and two legs, going to and coming from all different parts of the galaxy, with suitcases and bags. As a matter of fact, Lee could not believe how many humans there were.

"This looks like a regular airport," whispered Lee, "except ... with aliens. Hey, you guys, I just thought of something, since WE are on Arbee's planet that makes us ALIENS."

"I never thought of that," laughed Banjo.

They could hear the flights being announced over the speakers: "Space Flight 337, Starline Transport, now boarding for the Ingondis System at Gate 27-A. We will be departing on time. Please have your boarding passes ready. Thank you."

Suddenly, Sam realized something, "WAIT ... the time! What time is it?"

"Why do you need to know the time?" asked Banjo.

"Because, we have to be back on Earth by a certain time, or our parents will come home and find us not there," explained Samantha.

"Is that a problem?" asked Arbee.

"Oh, man," said Lee. "Sam is right! They are going to be home around midnight and if we are not there, they are going to freak out! Arbee, we aren't in the past where time goes slower. We are in the present, remember?"

"I see," said Arbee, as he rubbed his chin. "That completely slipped my mind."

"If we don't get back, our parents will call the police, and we will be in HUGE trouble," added Lee.

"Oh, my," said Arbee. "Alright then, we had better get you back to Earth and quickly."

The Science Team rushed out of the space port, got on an air taxicab, flew back to the shuttle. They got aboard and flew back to the starship. The repair crews had finished their work and had packed up and left some time ago.

"Wow, those repair guys work fast," said Sam.

Within minutes, Arbee and Zinzu had gotten the okay to take off. It was soon after that they were flying away from planet Izikzah and back to planet Earth at super-light speed.

"This is so cool," laughed Banjo. "We are going so fast that you can't even see the stars. So, how are you going to drop us off without being seen? You can't just fly us in a spaceship and let us out in front of our house. Our government has radar, and they will spot you for sure."

"Yeah," said Lee. "Then they will send fighter jets and shoot us out of the sky!"

"Do not worry," said Arbee. "I have a few tricks I can use to outsmart the Earth authorities. Just tell me what time I need to have you home and give me the directions to where you live, and let me take care of the rest."

"We need to be home by eleven at night," said Sam, "that's just to be safe."

"All set," said Arbee. "We will arrive at Planet Earth in about forty-five minutes. Meanwhile, let us load the new Protecto-Pod security system into the computer, shall we?"

The Science Team, Arbee, and Zinzu, gathered around a computer screen on the bridge. Arbee opened the box. It had ten of the red glass-like spheres in it, and a computer disk, just like Spido promised.

Arbee put the disk into the computer. The screen came on. There was a picture of a small, oval-shaped, multi-colored alien with four arms and two frog-like eyes. He spoke, "Congratulations, you are now the proud owners of a PROTECTO-POD-8000 Security System."

Banjo laughed. "Hey, Lee, even these guys have infomercials."

"Yeah," laughed Lee. "It's like alien cable TV."

"Your Protecto-Pod-8000 system will protect your ship

from any unwanted life forms, no matter what their size, strength, or number," said the alien on the screen.

"Just by inserting this computer disk in your computer, you have automatically set up your Protecto-Pod 8000 Security System. Each crew member on the ship must now say their name, so the Protecto-Pods do not throw you off your own ship. Ha, ha, ha," the alien joked.

"Oh, brother, this guy's a salesman and a comedian," laughed Sam.

Arbee, Zinzu, and each member of the Science Team spoke into the computer.

"Hey, what about Dino," said Banjo.

"Yeah, and Bootsey," added Sam. "I don't want him getting zapped."

Arbee picked up Bootsey and held him up to the computer.

"REEOWWW!" said Bootsey. "Put me down, you floating washing machine. I was sleeping," he thought.

Then Arbee brought Dino. "Speak, boy," said Arbee.

Dino just stared at him wagging his tail. "I am a dog. I can't speak," he thought.

"Biscuit, do you want a biscuit Dino?" asked Arbee.

"WOOF," went Dino. Arbee tossed him the biscuit.

"If that is your entire crew please say, 'Complete'," said

the salesman alien on the screen.

"Complete," said Arbee.

"Excellent! The Protecto-Pod 8000 now has both visual and sound recognition of all seven of your crew members," said the salesman. "To start your system, please say ... 'START'."

"Go ahead, Samantha," said Arbee.

"Oh ... okay," said Sam. "START!" she said loudly.

"YOU HAVE DONE IT! Your Protecto-Pod 8000 is now activated," said the alien.

Suddenly, the red spheres rose out of the box, into the air, and lit up.

"Look," said Sam. "They have got eyes."

"Yeah weird looking," laughed Lee. "More cool aliens!"

The spheres took off flying in all directions to guard different parts of the ship.

Dino saw them flying by and started barking wildly. He chased after one of the flying spheres. "A BALL!" he thought. Dino ran down the hall, barking all the way.

"Oh, no," Banjo groaned. "Dino thinks those things are tennis balls. He will be chasing after them for hours."

"Silly dog," thought Bootsey. "They are so easily fooled."

"Well, there you have it," said the sales alien. "Your Protecto-Pod 8000 is on the job. Remember our motto ... 'You sleep tight and let us fight.' Good bye, and thank you for choosing the Protecto-Pod 8000, the finest quality security system in the whole universe." The computer screen went off.

"Awesome," said Sam. She took he disc out and put it away.

"At last, a real security system," said Arbee. "No more pesky Deinonychus sneaking on our ship."

"And no more hostile life forms messing up our ship" agreed Zinzu. "Arbee, we are approaching the Planet Earth."

"Very well," said Arbee. "Bring us to the right position and time."

"Done," said Zinzu. "The time is 11 o'clock at night, Western Standard Time. We are located over their home town on the West Coast of North America."

"Good," said Arbee. "Science Team, please gather up Dino and meet me in the shuttle dock."

"A shuttle ... seriously ... we are taking a ... shuttle?" exclaimed Lee. "But Arbee, it's like I told you before ... the Air Force will blow us out of the sky!"

"Do not worry. I know a few tricks. I am an alien ... remember?" said Arbee. "Follow me."

After finally finding Dino, who had chased a Protecto-Pod to the other side of the ship, they all arrived in the starship's shuttle dock.

Arbee had them climb into a small craft. It was all black

and it even had black windows. It was a tight squeeze. Dino had to sit on Lee and Banjo's lap and Bootsey had to sit on Sam's lap.

"I hope this ride isn't going to be too long," thought Bootsey, "because I have got to pee. What do you people think I am, a water bottle?"

"Dog, you need to lose some weight," grumbled Lee.

"Silly people," thought Dino, "always worried about their figures and weight. I have the perfect dog figure, round and puffy."

"Here we go," said Arbee. He flew the black shuttle out of the starship and straight down to Earth. In less than five minutes, Arbee was hovering over the Science Team's neighborhood. The team could see their houses on a big view screen.

"Which one of these homes belongs to your family Banjo?" asked Arbee.

"Two houses up on the right ... there," said Banjo. "You should land in the back yard so that no one can see us. I would never be able to explain to the neighbors why we climbed out of a UFO."

Arbee floated the shuttle into Banjo's back yard and landed softly on the grass.

"How did you get by the Air Force?" asked Lee.

"They cannot shoot at what they cannot see," said Arbee. "There is no way that they can detect this shuttle craft or the starship. Now, off you go. I will see you all in two weeks."

"Samantha, I could use your help in three days to finish up the Deinonychus research," Arbee said.

"Sure, see you then," said Sam. "My math test isn't until next week."

They all climbed out of the black shuttle, except Banjo who gave Arbee a hug. "Thanks for saving me and Dino," said Banjo.

"Think nothing of it, my boy," said Arbee. "After all, what are friends for? I will see you all in two weeks."

"Woof!" barked Dino. "Yeah, thanks for saving me … and the good food, too," he thought.

"Well, being around you is never boring," thought Bootsey. "And thanks for saving the dog over here, but don't tell him I said that."

"I will not tell him," said Arbee

"'Bye, thanks," said Lee.

Arbee waved and then closed the door to the black craft without making a sound. The shuttle lifted off and silently disappeared into the nighttime sky.

The Science Team stumbled into Banjo's house. It was 11:05 exactly.

"How did he do it?" whispered Lee.

"Alien science," Sam sighed.

"Alien science," said Banjo. "I ... love ... it."

They were very tired and hungry so they all ate some of Mrs. Montgomery's Tons of Tuna Casserole, which tasted better than it looked.

"Hey, this stuff isn't so bad. It's kind of good," mumbled Lee. "These green things in here are peas ... right?"

They all went off to their rooms and fell into a deep sleep. It felt good to be home. It felt even better to be ... alive.

Later That Week

Sam went back through the doggy door time tunnel a few days later. When she came back, she told Lee and Banjo the strangest story.

"When Arbee flew his starship back in time to study the Deinonychus pack again," explained Sam, "he landed the ship in the same spot we were before and, guess what?"

"What?" asked Lee and Banjo.

"Scarface and the whole pack were there, waiting for him," said Sam, "right in the same place where we fed them the chicken."

"No way," whispered Lee.

"I swear," said Sam. "They were just standing there bobbing up and down like pigeons or chickens or something."

"I'll bet they wanted more chicken, huh?" said Banjo.

"Exactly," laughed Sam. "They came back for more chicken!"

"So, what did Arbee do?" asked Lee. "He can't feed them forever."

"Well, he fed them a bunch of chicken the first day, "said Sam, "but for the next week he fed them less and less until finally . . ."

"No more chicken," guessed Banjo.

"Yep," said Sam, "until there was no more chicken."

"Then what happened?" whispered Lee.

"Then Scarface and the others just left," said Sam. "I guess they figured that the food supply had run out and they went back to hunting regular dinosaurs."

"I'll bet all the plant-eaters liked it better when the Raptors were eating chicken," laughed Lee.

Banjo flopped back on his bed. "If I never see another piece of fried chicken again, it is okay with me," he sighed.

As usual, Dino and the Science Team are never very far from danger in:

Great Snoring Stegosaurs!

Look for the next Adventures of Dinosaur Dog – coming soon.

Just then many of the Stegosaurs made grunting noises and moved away from the Science Team, turning their spiked tails toward them.

"Move back everyone," said Arbee, "back away from their tails. Something is scaring them."

Dino heard the – CRACK– of a branch behind them. He turned around and "Grrrrrrr, arf, arf," he barked a warning, but it was too late. Dino saw some sort of feathered dinosaur leap into the air and – THUMP – land on the backpack that Banjo was wearing.

"AAAAH!" Banjo screamed and fell to the ground trying to knock the creature off of him.